Planning on Christmas

GEETA SCHRAYTER

PREMA PRESS

For my husband and my sister, for helping me prioritize writing
even when I considered it impossible among the chaos of life. I literally
could not have done this without you.

1

Death by frozen water was *not* on my to-do list.

The thought swirled through my mind as the car swirled on ice. My list was lengthy, they always were. But none of the color-coded items I scheduled to check off today included losing control of anything, let alone my car. Let alone my relationship. Yet here I was, single and spiraling, and it was pissing me the eff off.

I took my foot off the gas and jerked the wheel in the direction opposite the one I was heading, hoping to stop the spin. My headlights accented the falling snow in the dark—snow that started suddenly and without mercy—and the white flecks flew across my vision like a jostled snow globe I was begrudgingly in the middle of.

"Not a tree, not a tree, not a tree" was my plea as the car continued its solo routine. The country road was lined with them; they loomed on either side like an amused audience, waiting to see how the city girl handled an icy street. "I'm not just any city girl," I muttered to the wilderness as I jerked the wheel once more. "I'm Charity Fucking Evans."

The motion brought the car around so it was facing the road again, thank goodness, but I was on the downside of a hill, and the vehicle showed no signs of stopping its slide. I pressed lightly on the brake but the car fishtailed in answer, causing me to regret my decision to stick with the rear-wheel drive that came standard in my car. At the foot of the hill lights twinkled up at me, and my concern for striking timber shifted to buildings, cars, and possibly people.

"Shit!" I screamed to the void. "Damn you Darren!" After all, if he hadn't chosen such piss-poor timing for his out-of-the-blue announcement, I wouldn't have been speeding. I worked to keep the car on the road as it continued its slide.

"Damn you Hannigans!" After all, if Sarabeth and her Mother Dreadful listened to me and held the wedding in Boston instead of some god-forsaken manor in the country, I wouldn't be on this road.

"And damn you SNOW!" A name far too pleasant-sounding for what I was actually dealing with: frozen effing H2O.

The lights from the town grew brighter, and the car remained on its descent. I made a split second decision then, spun the wheel to the right, and braced myself as the perfect M5 I'd gifted myself when my company surpassed every goal I'd set last year dipped off the road I'd been trying so hard to keep it on. It came to a stop, complete with crunching noises that made me cringe, with its nose buried in a snowbank.

The impact jerked me forward, and my head slammed onto the steering wheel.

"Ouch. Fuck, fuck, fuck." I let out a breath and released the vice-like grip I had on the wheel, one of my hands coming to hold the spot on my head that immediately began to throb. "Okay. It's okay. We're okay."

This was actually an "I" situation, not a "we" scenario but that was beside the point. And honestly, I wasn't entirely sure if I meant I was okay because of what just happened or my new relationship status, but I'd have to save more thorough musings for later. Another deep breath.

"Alright. Next move." I picked up my phone and attempted to call roadside assistance, but when the call wouldn't go through, I noticed the lack of service. "That's the country for you."

I rolled my eyes at no one and grabbed my bag from the backseat, which was large enough for my laptop, planner, and multiple notebooks. I'd never be able to get behind the use of anything smaller —too many necessities. I pulled on my coat and stepped from the car. Snow pelted my face immediately and I brought the faux-fur lined hood up for some protection. I checked to make sure my car was safely off the road, not that there was much I could do if it wasn't, and glanced toward the lights at the bottom of the hill. I took a deep breath, and did the only thing left to do: walk.

❄❄❄

The heavy wooden door opened with a chime that seemed

superfluous; the sound of the bell was surely drowned out by the din of music and low chatter. Warmth reached me immediately, and I resisted the urge to shake the snow from my shoulders like some kind of animal. My eyes swept around the small restaurant: it was a comforting combination of cream walls with black accents and rich wood. White fairy lights surrounded the windows and ran along the edge of the ceiling and the wood bar off to one side. A fireplace flickered in the dining room. Most of the tables were occupied—a surprise considering the weather—but I wasn't in a dinner-for-one mood anyway, so I hung my coat on the hanger by the door, took a seat on one of the black stools, and smiled at the bartender.

"Well hello there," she said brightly, her eyebrow raising just a tad. Perhaps unfamiliar snowstorm guests weren't a commodity. "What can I get for you?"

"Hmm," I picked up the drink menu she placed in front of me. Not one for indecisiveness, I scanned the names and settled on the first to jump out. "I'll have a Gin-gle Bell Rock."

I took out one of my notebooks along with my pouch of colored pens. While the bartender worked her magic, I got to work addressing the situation at hand. I was more frazzled than I cared to admit, but knew putting everything on paper would help sort it out; each line on my list would feel like a mental tangle coming undone. I selected a color not yet in use: orange seemed appropriate for the emergency-like situation.

> *–Call tow truck*
> *–Get car towed*
> *–Assess damage*
> *–Schedule repairs*
> *–Rent car if needed*
> *–Get to Juniper Manor ASAP*

Another color for Darren. It was a shame I didn't have chartreuse, but I settled for yellow.

> *–Get belongings*

I hovered for a moment, poised to add more, but when I drew a blank, I decided I'd circle back to that particular topic and focused instead on the other items to add, which already had their designated hue. Blue was reserved for tasks related to company events, and my priority was reaching out to my assistant.

-Text Natalie

I looked around and uttered a silent prayer when I found a chalkboard sign with wifi information. I paused to send her a text as the bartender dropped off my drink.

Me: Do not be alarmed, but I'm going to be late.

It was the best I could do. I had no clue how long it'd take me to get everything else sorted, but Natalie was a bit more excitable than I was, and I didn't want her flying off the rails. I needed her calm, cool, and collected until I got there. The Hannigans were borderline Boston royalty, and the wedding of their sole daughter was my company's biggest event of the year, one that would inevitably lead to more considering the family's political involvement and charitable tendencies. Both things screamed "events." It had to go off without a hitch, and my not being there exactly when I said I would could be perceived as exactly that unless I handled this right.

If I didn't know Natalie was expecting me at the manor in—I glanced at my watch—half an hour, I wouldn't have bothered to message. *Fix issues before anyone else gets involved and inevitably makes the situation messier than it needs to be.* One of my mottos.

I took a sip of my drink and tried not to visibly sputter at the strength of the cocktail. It sounded good on paper: gin meets holiday punch, but the bartender did *not* go light on said gin. Still, it would probably do me some good. My exterior might appear calm—an art I'd perfected—but my body was tense from the crash, a to-do list that wasn't being followed . . . and Darren.

I took another sip, grimaced, and urged my muscles to relax. But also, fuck him. I scratched off "text Natalie" with a bit more force than necessary, and took a moment to enjoy the satisfaction I felt at completing something. Honestly, working my way through lists was endorphin-inducing.

Another sip, and another grimace.

"Not a fan?"

I turned toward the voice to find a man sitting two stools over, sporting an amused grin that had one dimple flexing. His arms rested on the bar, the sleeves of his white button-down rolled to his elbows. One hand cradled a rocks glass filled with an amber liquid that seemed to match the hue of his twinkling eyes.

"It sounded good on paper but . . . " I shrugged.

"Really? Toni's usually spot on. You want me to tell her to make you a new one?" The man turned like he was about to get the bartender's attention, but I quickly leaned over and stopped him with a hand on his arm.

"No, no!"

His gaze flicked to my hand, and I removed it as quick as I'd placed it there—not fast enough to avoid acknowledging said arm was quite toned beneath that button-down though.

"Sorry," I apologized for my knee-jerk reaction. "It's not bad, it's just strong."

"Ah, now that sounds like Toni," he said with a not-unattractive smirk.

"I should have gone with my usual and ordered a glass of wine. Oh well. Cheers!" I lifted the cocktail again and took another drink. A few more and I wouldn't mind the strength, but I had to be careful: there was still work to be done. Then again, there was *always* work to be done. That's what it took to stay ahead. To be on top. Which was precisely the position I preferred.

I turned my attention back to my notebooks and the list of things left to do for the wedding. My phone chimed then, and I checked Natalie's response.

Natalie: That's unlike you. Everything ok?

Me: YEP!

I had to admit, Natalie knew me pretty well. She paid attention, which boded well for her future. I added a smiling emoji to my response for good measure, then deleted it for fear of overkill. She'd catch that. I turned back to my friendly companion, who'd started chatting with Toni. I cleared my throat and Toni gave a nod my way to redirect his attention.

"Hi, me again. Sorry to bother you but I actually have a slight prob —"

The door to the restaurant burst open, and I forgot what I was about to say as a gust of wind and snow swirled around a looming figure who filled the doorway.

2

The figure decked in full snow gear including balaclava rushed to the bar.

"Kyle. KYLE. We have an emergency situation," he said as he pulled off the mask which caused his grayish-brown hair to stick in all different directions.

"Kyle" turned out to be Mr. Amber Eyes, who spun on the stool and gave the newcomer his full attention.

"What is it, George?"

"I was trying to get another layer of sand down the main stretch before things really pick up tonight." The man ran a hand across his head, partially taming his wild hair.

Before things really pick up?? What did they consider the current weather?

"There's a car off the road up Dog Hill." George continued in a rush, his arms flailing animatedly around him. "A sporty one crashed in the snow, definitely not meant for this weather. I pulled over to see if I could help, but it's empty. No sign of anyone. Not even a footprint left in this. Call a search party! Maybe they're lost and hurt and near frozen!"

The noise in the restaurant died down at George's outburst, and I was grateful for the low lighting—I was positive my cheeks were on fire.

"That won't be necessary, George."

"Whatta you MEAN?! They could be anywhere!"

"Yes, they could be," Kyle let out a chuckle, and I was about to chalk him up as a sociopath for not caring about another human being when he turned his gaze back on me, that dimple even deeper than before.

7

"But I'm pretty sure 'anywhere,' is right here. It's you, isn't it?"

I bit my lip and nodded. Cheeks most definitely cherry red. "Guilty. How'd you guess?"

He gave a noncommittal shrug. "It's an odd time for a newcomer around these parts. Everything is fine, folks," he spoke in the general direction of the dining room, and the chatter once again picked up.

"I um, mean to take care of the car. It's on my list." I tapped my notebook. "Can you recommend a good tow?"

"First things first: are you okay? George said 'crash.'"

I grimaced as I remembered the sound my poor car made when it hit the bank, and my hand flew reflexively to my forehead. There was admittedly still a slight throb, but the drink was helping in that department.

"I'm fine. I lost control on the ice, and when I saw I was headed for an occupied area I took it off the road."

He tilted his head and raised an eyebrow. "Took it off the road?"

I sat straighter. "Yes. I attempted to regain control, but once I got the car facing the right direction it became clear I wasn't going to be able to stop it. It was sliding. I've never been here before and didn't know what I'd find at the bottom or if I'd be able to steer it safely and keep from hitting a building or, god forbid, an actual person, so I made a call."

I looked from George, to Kyle, then over at Toni who stopped cocktail crafting to listen, her tattooed arms crossed in front of her chest. It was a silent dare to the lot of them: go ahead and make a snide comment about women drivers. Thankfully, none came. After a beat, Toni gave me a nod that seemed to say "atta girl," and Kyle chuckled lightly.

"Well George, there you have it. All's well; our guest seems to have everything under control. Sit down and have yourself a drink—non-alcoholic, of course—before you head back out. The snow will be there when you're through." He gave George a friendly pat on the shoulder. "As for you, ms . . . ?"

"Charity. Charity Evans."

I held out a hand and he clasped it for a shake, his grip warm and firm.

"Ms. Evans. Paul over there—" Kyle hooked a thumb over his shoulder. "He's the tow truck driver, but his garage closed for the night so as you can see, he's begun his imbibing. And that fact aside, not even tow trucks are immune to weather conditions."

I looked at the man sitting across from a laughing woman, their table laden with food and drink. Shit.

"He's the only one?"

"Afraid so," Kyle gave me an apologetic look.

"Can I drive it?"

He'd been mid sip, and nearly choked on his drink. "Drive what??"

"The tow truck, of course." I wasn't one for sitting around idly.

"Do you drive tow trucks often?"

"No, but I have somewhere to be. I'm a quick study."

"No offense Ms. Evans—"

"Charity is fine."

"Charity. But have you looked outside?"

I glanced out one of the windows, framed in those festive lights, and saw snowfall so fast and thick it created a curtain of white, apparent even in the dark of night.

"Damnit. Think it will let up soon? I could just wait it out here and then go back for my car. I'm sure it's only a little stuck. I could probably dig it out with a shovel if there's one around here I could borrow . . . " I started to turn in my chair like I might find one leaning up against a wall.

"Ms. Evans—"

"Charity."

"Charity." He chuckled again, which would usually make my hackles rise as I assumed it was in mockery, but Kyle didn't give off that vibe. He seemed amused, sure, but also a bit in awe. "You're formidable. I can see that. Under different circumstances, I'm sure Paul would be more than happy to let you try your hand at his tow. And while there are plenty of shovels, I'm not sure that's such a great idea right now. Where have you been the last week and a half? News coverage has been almost exclusively about this storm."

I bit my lip. Focused on the Hannigan wedding, that's where. Watching The Weather Channel wasn't typically on my to-do list, at least not with outdoor event season over. And even when people were all about celebrations en plein air, Natalie usually kept tabs on the weather which was why . . . oh.

A conversation where Natalie *strongly* urged me to drive up the day before came to mind. The word "snow" may or may not have been included in said urging, but I'd waved her off. Literally. I'd given her a dismissive wave, as I simultaneously flipped through my notebook, started typing out an email, and made a phone call. Then I sent her to keep tabs on things. Everything was in order for the wedding, I'd said. It'd be *fine*, I'd said, and I'd get more done if I hung back and drove the next day. Today. Well damn.

"I um, may have been aware some snow was expected." I cleared my throat. "I thought I could beat it."

George leaned forward so his face appeared in front of Kyle's. "Some snow!? This is predicted to be as bad as Nemo!"

"Er . . . "

"He means a snowstorm from 2013," Kyle clarified. "The one that brought some of the most snowfall since the blizzard of 1888."

"Mix that with some wind, and the speed of that storm from '03 and phewww! It's gonna be a doozy." George's eyes grew wide as he mentioned it, as awareness seemed to set in. "Speaking of which, I better get back out with the boys. It's gonna be quite the night."

I had my own moment of awareness then, as George pushed himself off the stool, gave a nod, and was gone in another gust of wind and snow: what about the wedding?! What would this storm mean for the freaking wedding of the year?!

I swiveled back to Kyle. "I've really got somewhere I need to be. What are the chances I can get to Monroe tonight?"

He shook his head. "Not very good I'm afraid. You're still about two hours out, and that's on a day the roads aren't turning into an ice rink."

Damnit. Okay. Pivot. I could pivot.

"I'm going to assume waiting it out in the restaurant isn't going to work, either?"

Another shake of the head. "Not expected to end soon enough for that."

I turned to my notebook and added "book hotel room" to my orange list.

"Ugh. This is not how I planned for the day to go."

"Well you can't control everything, you know? Definitely not the weather."

I looked over at him, fire in my green eyes. "I can sure as hell try." I took back the rest of my drink and slammed the glass on the bar for emphasis. "And besides, haven't you heard of cloud seeding? Weather can, in fact, be modified."

Kyle followed suit and finished his drink in solidarity. "Modified and controlled are two different things."

"Perhaps, but through said modification you're adjusting things in an attempt to get an outcome you desire—to make something happen the way you want it to happen, no? In other words, control it."

"I like your reasoning, but I still wouldn't say they're the same. Besides, that science is used to make more rain or snow. As far as I know there's no way to make less—to stop a snowstorm from happening at all. So again I say, you can't control everything."

His logic displeased me. How could it not? I didn't like to think about the things outside my control. The variables. They led to the worst things in life.

Images of my father flitted through my mind: healthy dad, sick but hopeful dad, a dad so tired he could no longer hide it, that bright smile shaky and wavering. I couldn't control his illness. I got to stand by and watch it steal him.

Images of my mother flew past next: happy mom, worried but hopeful mom, a mom so sad she could no longer hide it, that bright smile fleeting and rare. I couldn't control her feelings. I got to stand by and watch as she broke.

My lack of control in those areas led me to find ways to regulate elsewhere, and honestly, it changed my life. I remember feverishly distracting myself; going up to my room to avoid the hushed whispers and heartbreak that became standard in our home post-diagnosis. I was 10. They tried to hide it at first, but I knew. Tears streamed down my face as I looked around my messy space for something, anything, to occupy myself with. To *do* something. I focused my attention on cleaning, then rearranged and reorganized. Afterwards, I sat in the middle of my perfectly ordered bedroom and felt . . . calm. The chaos in my heart and home felt settled. *I did this,* I thought. I relished that feeling, and knew I'd do whatever it took to keep it with me.

Next summer led to the famous lemonade stand for cancer research. I made list after list of all I needed to do. We built the stand, which was still in my mom's basement. Dad felt well enough that day to help my younger brother Caleb and me make it. No one said it would be our last real project together, but the reality hung over the endeavor like a thundercloud. I made the lemonade, and marketing to go with it, which I set up days in advance. I put an ad in the local paper. I fired my best friend at the time because our artistic visions didn't align, and figured out how to include Caleb per mom's request while keeping him out of my way: his job was adding ice to the cups. And even said ice was a strategic move, as ice in cups equaled less lemonade which equaled more profit. Of course, I advertised it as though it was solely for the customers' benefit. "Ice cold lemonade" went over well.

Funnily enough, I remember checking the weather then. I knew I needed a hot, sunny day for the best ROI—a term dad taught me—and it didn't disappoint. I made so much money, Jack's Lemonade ended up on the news.

If only I'd thought to check the weather this time . . .

I allowed silence to hang for a beat, then changed the subject.

"How come this place is still so busy? If the roads are that bad, and only going to get worse, why isn't everyone at home? Is there a hotel I can check into nearby?"

He shrugged. "Most of us are used to the snow. Nothing some good ol' 4-wheel drive and caution can't handle. But most live nearby, too. Some of these folks are in walking distance. I'm sure the weather will have even the bravest heading out before long, though. And as for a hotel, well, there isn't one."

"What!"

"Auburn Falls is no ski town. Either you live here like me, or you're just passing through like you."

I bit my lip again. Auburn Falls. I'd never even heard of it. The last sign I remembered seeing was for a town called Riverdale. This pitstop was not on any list of mine, and I continued to be displeased with the lack of control. In fact, it made me feel like I might hyperventilate. I held up my glass as cue for Toni to make another.

"Do you think I'll get arrested if I sleep in my car?"

"Well no . . . " Kyle drawled. "I've done it a few times myself over the years after a long night at this very bar, or a party in the woods in my youth, but it's too cold for that." He looked contemplative for a minute. "Look, we may not have a hotel, but I know a place you can stay."

I raised an eyebrow. "I'm not going home with you, if that's what you're insinuating. You're practically a stranger! I don't have time to watch shows but I've heard about those murder docs that are all the rage; I'm not looking to get my own episode. I'm flattered, though."

He let out a deep laugh. "That wasn't supposed to be a pick-up line."

"Oh." I turned to focus on the drink Toni slid over, picking it up and taking a lengthy sip. As expected, the second went down much easier.

"I mean, it's not you. I just don't make a habit of taking home women I just met. Now, helping them find a place to stay when they're stranded in a snowstorm? That I can do. Where were you headed anyway?"

I took another drink and tried to make my embarrassment go down with the alcohol. "Juniper Manor."

"Ah. I should have guessed."

I turned back to him and started slightly at the reaction his amber eyes caused. "Is it that obvious?"

"Well, in Monroe it's gotta be either there or Pine Ridge, and something tells me you're not here for the slopes."

"That obvious, too?"

He gave me a slow once over, taking in my cream-colored cashmere sweater, sleek dark wash jeans, and black, heeled ankle boots. Perhaps I should have felt bothered by his lengthy gaze—I'd certainly given other men an earful for much less—but I didn't. Instead, I realized I felt heat that didn't come from the gin at his study. Was this normal? My boyfriend of seven years literally *just* broke up with me. I hadn't even fully processed what that jerk had done, yet here I was, relishing the look of a near stranger.

Kyle gave a tiny shake of his head, as though he hadn't meant to look so long, and cleared his throat.

"A little," he said, running a hand through his brown hair and letting that grin return. "Anyway, have you eaten? The shepherd's pie is delicious. Grab a bite then I'll bring you somewhere to stay for the night. It's not far. I just have a quick meeting to get to."

As though he was a stage director and that was the cue, the door opened again and a group of people entered. Kyle stood to greet them, leaving me at the bar with a friendly wink and a flutter, wondering what sort of meeting took place at 6 p.m. in a snowstorm. I watched as he led them to a table in the dining room.

Nope, nope, nope. Nothing about the way this evening had gone or looked like it was headed was going according to plan. I picked up one of my pens and let it hover over the page in my notebook, poised to add the next item on my list. But for the first time in a long while—20 years worth of "long while"—I was unsure what to write. So with an exasperated sigh I tossed down my writing utensil and ordered the shepherd's pie.

3

I opened the door to Kyle's truck and climbed in with a full belly—the meal had in fact been delicious—and a mood much more relaxed thanks to Toni's concoctions. The vehicle roared to life, and as we pulled out of the parking lot and the headlights illuminated the road, my eyes widened at the amount of snow already on the ground. This wasn't my first winter. I was a Boston girl now, after all, but for some reason it felt like so much more out here, with fewer lights, buildings, vehicles, and people. There was more wilderness. More space to fill with white.

I shivered slightly from the cold, a movement Kyle noticed, because he turned the heat on high and pressed a button for the seat warmer.

"Thank you," I offered up.

His truck was clean—I suppose I wasn't surprised—and smelled like cinnamon and pine.

"It smells . . . "

"Like Christmas?" he finished with a grin as his truck drove along as though the roads weren't covered in the same substance that made me crash my M5 just hours earlier. I almost whimpered at the thought. My poor car.

"I was going to say cinnamon and pine," I laughed. "But I guess Christmas is true too."

"'Tis the season!"

"I suppose it is."

"Why don't you sound sure?"

I shrugged, "I don't usually do much celebrating. Too busy."

"Too busy for Christmas?" He seemed genuinely appalled. "Seems to me that means you're too busy. Period."

I mulled his statement over as he turned the truck up a long drive. Was there such a thing as 'too busy'? I didn't think so. We all had the same number of hours in a day, but the difference between me and others who wished they could accomplish all I had was mismanagement. Sitting around. Letting minutes slip by without applying them.

Time is wild. It needs to be tamed. Managed. Organized. Utilized. Every day we make choices as far as what to do with the minutes we're given. Some choose to let them stay unruly, zipping by like there's no other way. But others—like myself—choose a more proactive approach. And so far, it's served me well. I decided then I didn't like the word "busy." Most people said it with a negative connotation, but the way I kept my schedule was exactly the way I liked it. I wasn't 'busy,' I was 'purposefully occupied.' There. How much better did that sound? Wording was everything. I opened my mouth to tell Kyle, but before I had a chance he put the truck in park.

"We're here."

"Oh!"

Through the rapidly swishing wipers and the curtain of snow highlighted by the headlights, I could just make out a house in front of us. The door opened, and warm light spilled into the winter night, silhouetting the figure of a woman.

"That'll be Mary." Kyle looked down at his watch. "I've got to get going, but she'll take care of you."

"Oh, ok." I was surprised by the dip of disappointment I felt at his not staying to walk me in, but I quickly shoved it aside and gave him a bright smile. "Well, thanks for everything. I appreciate it so much."

I held out my hand and he took it with the amused expression— crooked grin, dimple, amber eyes I could tell were twinkling even in the dark—that I decided was a signature look. I didn't hate it.

"You're welcome Ms. Evans."

I opened the door and stepped out of the truck, my feet disappearing into the snow.

"Charity," I said in mock annoyance. "Goodbye Kyle."

I closed the door and started to walk toward the stranger's home, wondering what I'd gotten myself into, but paused as Kyle's voice carried through the snow.

"Charity!"

I turned to see he'd lowered the passenger side window.

"That goodbye sounded awful final. I don't want to mislead, so I wanted to make sure you knew you'll be seeing me again." The proclamation caused an unexpected flutter of excitement. "There's the matter of your car. Plus—" he nodded toward the woman in the doorway. "That's my mom."

Of course it was. Looks like he'd brought me home, after all.

❄❄❄

As soon as I opened my eyes, I knew something was wrong. It wasn't the fact I was in an entirely unfamiliar place—a bedroom that looked straight from Pottery Barn's holiday collection—with delicious breakfast smells creeping under the door. No, it was the fact I woke up to silence. No alarm. When's the last time that happened? And more importantly, WHY had that happened?

The blinds were drawn on the windows, but I could tell it was morning, even though the light peeking around the edges was somewhat muted. Was it still snowing?

I turned over, allowed myself to admit the bed was *really* comfortable, and came face-to-face with a clock on the bedside table. My eyes widened as I registered the position of the hands. 9:30. It couldn't be. I picked it up and brought it closer to my face, blinking hard, but the hands remained rooted in place.

NINE THIRTY?! I flipped back over and picked up my phone from the opposite table, dismayed to find the battery died in the night.

Why oh why hadn't I taken all my things when I left the car? Leaving my charger behind felt like a rookie move. To be fair, I *had* been in the process of addressing phone battery insecurity by ordering a battery back-up, but the one-day delivery promise hadn't been fulfilled. I had a car charger, and was expecting to go from vehicle to manor, so I'd packed my other one in my suitcase. I tried to picture myself coming down that hill dragging all my luggage and cringed at the image. As it was, the snowy descent in my heeled boots had been a slippery mess. More ice skating than stepping.

I got out of bed, and as my feet touched the wood floor I noticed the fuzzy snowflake socks I'd been given. Mary had insisted.

"You'll thank me in the morning, this old house gets pretty drafty," she'd said.

It was true; now that I wasn't under a layer cake of blankets, I could feel cool air on my legs between where the socks ended and the flannel nightgown began—another insistence of hers.

I stood and looked at myself in the full-sized mirror that hung on one of the walls. My blonde hair was piled on top of my head in a lopsided bun. I still had on makeup from the day before—I never did that—and I looked . . . well, very much *not* like myself, in fuzzy socks and knee-length nightgown, framed by a bedroom that was decidedly festive. A garland hung over the wooden headboard, an evergreen pillow with prancing reindeer complemented plaid navy sheets, and mini decorative trees, snow globes, candles, and all the cozy blankets surrounded me.

I looked around for my clothes, then remembered Mary took them to wash. I offered up a silent prayer she'd know how to handle cashmere.

When I greeted her last night, I'd tried to keep my usual confident, can-do attitude and "tall girl" energy about me. At 5'8", the latter was something I'd been said to possess on more than one occasion, and while I could never say for certain whether it was supposed to be a compliment or an insult, I decided to think of it as the former no matter the speaker's intentions. But it was admittedly humbling and a bit awkward heading up a stranger's steps in the middle of the night.

Mary, however, was quick to ease my mind. She waited for me with a giant smile and the same twinkling eyes as her son. She ushered me into her home, settled me in the living room beside the fire, and handed me a mug of steaming mulled cider.

I felt like I was in another world entirely. Or a movie—one of those cheesy Christmas ones, perhaps. Was this Mrs. Claus? I'd shaken my head in a bit of disbelief.

"So what brings you to Auburn Falls?" she'd begun.

"I was on my way to Juniper Manor when the weather got the best of me . . . that's not something I typically allow to happen."

"Hmm," she mused as she a sipped her drink. "Well you can't control everything. Certainly not the weather."

"Your son said the same thing. Don't take this the wrong way, but I tend to think people who say 'you can't control everything' only do so because they don't have a handle on their life."

It was a comment that garnered another sip and contemplative "hmmm."

"Anyways," I continued hurriedly—the last thing I wanted was to insult my hostess. "Thank you so much for letting me spend the night, I promise I'll be out of your hair first thing in the morning."

"I wouldn't count on it dear, but it's not an issue, really."

"I don't think you understand: I *need* to be out of here first thing in the morning. I really have to get to the manor."

She shrugged nonchalantly. "We'll see what tomorrow brings, but this storm isn't supposed to stop until Sunday."

"Sunday?! No, no, no. I have an event Sunday!" I felt my pulse quicken the way it had at the restaurant. "Surely the town crew—George and them, will be out tomorrow. Paul will be back to work and can help get my car out. Or I can get a rental."

Mary gave me a sympathetic look from her place across from me, nestled in a high backed, dark green chair that mirrored my own. I wondered if she left them out all year. They felt like something Mr. and Mrs. Claus would settle in, especially with the decorative pillows, and cozy throws tossed over the back.

"You've already met some other residents, I see. They're hard workers, admittedly, but that may not be enough if Mother Nature decides so, at least not as fast as you're hoping. And there's no car rental in Auburn Falls. Drink your cider," she urged.

I'd listened, and as the warm drink full of spices, a subtle sweetness, and the taste of apples and rum slid down my throat I found myself able to relax. She showed me up to my room soon after, and left me with an "everything happens how it's meant to" which made me roll my eyes. Thankfully I was behind her so she didn't see.

That became my least favorite phrase when my dad was sick and a friend dared utter it. When a loved one is dying, that's probably one of the worst fucking things you could hear. I preferred "everything happens as you plan it" or, heck, even some good old fashioned "you reap what you sow." How about a little—or a lot—of control over one's destiny? *That's* what I was all about.

Now with a new day in front of me to try and get things in order, I walked to the window, pulled open the blind, and let out a gasp. I'd thought it looked like a lot of snow last night in the dark, but this? Put all the songs and sayings about snow all together and maybe that'd explain what I was looking at. Except for the phrase "winter wonderland." Leave that one out because I was currently less than pleased about the scene in front of me. "Wonderland" was a term I refused to apply to it, and the snow hadn't even stopped! It continued to fall steadily.

My window looked over a large front yard surrounded by trees. If there wasn't a gap between them that gave me a clue, I'd have no idea where the driveway was. Everywhere I looked, all I saw was white.

"Crap," I muttered.

With nothing more to do in the bedroom, I grabbed my bag and useless phone—a state that needed to be remedied ASAP—and followed the trail of breakfast scents to the kitchen.

4

Mary stood over the stove, and the sizzle of bacon mixed with the sound of classic Christmas tunes. She didn't notice me right away, so I went to stand by the wood-topped island and let my eyes roam the kitchen. It was a beautiful space: white cabinets and a white tile backsplash joined white marble counters, and it was all illuminated by that cursed snowy world outside thanks to a number of windows—my favorite was arched and sat behind the deep farmhouse sink. Despite the monochrome design choice, the room felt warm, inviting, and festive thanks to Mary's decorations.

Copper pots and pans hung over the island, and above them, boughs of pine and twinkling lights. A pine garland with more fairy lights hung over the arched window; a decorative tree sat in a ceramic pot beside the sink, and a wreath with a red velvet bow hung on the hood above the range. More pops of red were scattered about: a nutcracker cookie jar and Santa mugs, a sign that read "North Pole express," a bright red dutch oven, and a plaid runner. It was the sort of attention to detail I might apply to my own home if I were there enough to enjoy it, but it was hardly more than a place to sleep and shower. As a result, I kept my apartment open house ready. It looked like a staged home, to be honest.

"Oh! You're up!" Mary said when she turned around. "Are you hungry? I'm making breakfast sandwiches for the boys and there's plenty to be had. Take a seat."

I pulled out one of the stools surrounding the island. "The boys?"

"Yes, the town crew. They've been at it all night, and Auburn Falls being the size that it is, we don't exactly have a large employee rotation, so they'll be working straight through the storm."

"But you just said yourself it's not a big town. Has it really been all that bad?"

Mary gave me a look. It wasn't an unkind one, but it was certainly a bit "shows what you know," and as someone who prided themselves on *knowing*, I wasn't a fan of the expression.

"I take it you don't have much of an understanding about public works and snow removal?"

"Well, no. But what's there to understand? They just keep making passes to clear the snow as it piles up and put down salt and sand, right?"

"Something like that." Mary slid a steaming mug in front of me like the night before, this time filled with coffee, and motioned to a tray in the center of the island with sugar and a carafe full of cream. "They do their best. The priority is always keeping the main stretch clear, and then a single pass down the center of each road for emergency access. There's about 150 miles of road in town. It can take up to 8 hours to clear them all once a storm has passed. And as you can see . . . " she nodded toward the windows, "it hasn't passed yet."

"So you're telling me the roads aren't really drivable yet?"

She shook her head. "No, and in fact an alert was sent via the town's notification system encouraging residents to stay home as much as possible for their safety and to keep the roads clear for the crews. Of course, that's not to say everyone will listen; we've our fair share of individuals who think their driving skills exempt them. I just pray no one gets hurt.

"This is not good." I added a splash of cream to my coffee and took a sip. It didn't sit well in my stomach. Or perhaps that was just anxiety at my predicament.

"It's winter in New England, dear."

"I know, but it usually doesn't work against me like this."

"Weather doesn't work for or against anyone—it just is."

"Be that as it may, it's really not helping my company right now. You wouldn't happen to have a spare charger, would you? I left mine in the car and really need to reach out to my assistant."

Natalie was probably flipping the eff out.

"Of course!"

Mary got me squared away, and I pulled out my notebook while I waited for my phone to turn back on, more to give myself something to do than anything else. Idle hands and all. But I soon realized there was nothing else to list. Frustrated, I put down my pen and looked up at Mary hard at work mixing some sort of batter.

"Can I help?"

She immediately beamed at me, and I chided myself for not asking immediately.

"That would be wonderful! Here: could you start toasting these for me? Once they're done place them in that bowl and cover them with the tea towel to keep warm."

I walked over to where she motioned and started adding English muffins to a toaster oven.

"So . . . " I began after a few silent moments staring at bread. "Thank you again—so much—for letting me to stay here. If I'm being honest, I feel . . . well . . . "

How did I feel? Annoyed? Disoriented? Vulnerable? Anxious? I was a mix of them all, if I was being honest with myself—which I always tried to be. It was *sharing* those truths I wasn't necessarily a fan of. Keep up that mask: everything is under control. *I've* got everything under control.

"Well-rested, all things considered." I decided I'd skip a delve into my deeper feels. "You let a total stranger into your home in the middle of the night. Bold move. Foolish even, but I'm grateful you did."

"Well, you had Kyle speak in your favor. He's a good man, and that says a lot."

I bit my lip. Kyle. I'd momentarily forgotten about him. Not that he was forgettable, I just had a way of compartmentalizing and pushing aside unrelated—"

"Aw, mom, it's nice to know you speak so highly of me when you think I'm not around."

I jumped at the sound of his voice. He walked in the room, gave his mom a kiss on the cheek then smiled in my direction. And damn if that grin wasn't as cute as I'd found it the night before. I smiled back.

"Morning," he dipped his head slightly. "You look cozy."

In the presence of only Mary I forgot what I was wearing. But oh, how I remembered then. I looked down at the holly berries that adorned the nightgown, with its red button-front placket, tiny red bow, and lace hem. I was sure the hue of my cheeks changed to match the festive colors. My hand wanted to fly to my head where I knew my lopsided bun still sat, but I kept it firmly at my side, head held high. True, it wasn't my normal pulled-together ensemble, but my strength stemmed from much more than a killer outfit. I made my eyes meet Kyle's and allowed my smile to widen.

"Oh, I am, thank you! Mary gave me everything I needed to have a pleasant sleep last night, and was kind enough to wash my clothes for me."

"Ah, that reminds me! Take the eggs out when the timer goes off" she said and disappeared down the hall.

Kyle grabbed one of the Santa mugs and poured some coffee. He leaned against the counter, crossed his ankles, took a sip after adding cream and sugar, and looked at me with . . . was that mirth? I almost shook my head at the word that sprang to mind. MIRTH?! It felt like something that should only be applicable to children or Christmas characters, yet it flew immediately to mind when I looked at him. It fit.

But frankly, I wasn't sure what was so funny. It was just a nightgown. I opened my mouth to say so when a timer beeped, causing me to turn to the oven instead and take out a tray of eggs baked in tins—the cheese already melted on top.

"Shall we?" Kyle put down his mug, stepped beside me, and got to work assembling the sandwiches; he handed me a small spatula, took a square of aluminum foil from a pile Mary cut and set aside, added half a toasted English muffin, then motioned for me to add one of the eggs.

Afterwards, he reached in front of me to grab some bacon, and I inhaled the scent of fresh air, pine, and cedar. It was delicious. Refreshing. Uplifting. And, I realized, probably the result of his *actually* being outside rather than some fancy cologne. I gave my head a mental shake. Thinking about the way he smelled and what he was or wasn't doing this morning was *not* something I needed to do. No distractions. Too much else to think about.

"So, Ms. Evans—" he began as he finished the first sandwich and wrapped it up.

"It's Cha—"

"Right, right. Charity." There was that grin again. "So you say you slept well?"

"I did, actually. A bit too well I think. I can't believe how late I slept in. My phone died so of course I had no alarm. It's been a really long time since I woke without being serenaded by Bill Withers."

"Bill Withers, ey? Interesting choice."

I shrugged. "My dad's favorite."

"It's gonna be a lovely day," he said, and I couldn't help but smile at his knowing exactly the tune I was referring to.

My phone sounded once, twice, three times then, alerting me it'd turned back on, and I abandoned my station at the counter and rushed over.

"If I don't get to the manor, I doubt it," I said like he was referring to the actual day instead of a song.

Messages from Natalie. I expected as much.

Natalie: Ok seriously, are you alright?

Charity?

Where are you?

I'm worried. DO I CALL SOMEONE?!

The texts were hours apart, the last from earlier this morning. An image of Natalie curled up in the corner of her room freaking out over what to do flitted through my mind. But no. No, I had to give her more credit than that. That only happened once, and it wasn't a hotel room, it was the corner of her office. There'd been a lot going on, and I refused to hold it against her. Especially since I'd had my own panic attack not that long ago, and she'd been right there to help me. She was a dedicated, diligent worker, and her occasional flightiness was managed by my lists. I'd sent her with lots. All she had to do was remember to breathe and follow them.

"Do you mind if I answer this?"

"Go right ahead, this isn't my first rodeo when it comes to sandwich assembly."

I sat at the island, flipped through my notebook to copies of all I'd given Natalie, and worked my way backwards to today.

Friday. Most of the guests should have arrived already. It'd been suggested they check in Thursday, as Sarabeth and her mother wanted everyone rested for today's festivities. Assuming they arrived earlier in the day like Natalie—and unlike me—they'd be set to experience a day full of activities at the manor: the spa, the game room, the indoor pool, afternoon paint and sips, a cocktail crafting class, cards and cigars, and more. There was definitely something for everyone.

I didn't think anyone I hired for the event following my standard, rigorous interview process would be thrown by some snow, and for that I was grateful. I was certain the manor staff, headed by a manager who seemed more than competent, would be prepared for this sort of thing as well, being a venue in the mountains.

I thought about what to tell Natalie for a moment, and decided on optimism.

> **Me:** Morning Nat! Experienced a bit of a snow delay. Hoping to get there soon.

I looked out the window and admittedly felt uncertain about that last part, what with the snow still swirling through the air, but I sent the message anyway. Those three dots appeared almost immediately, and I watched as they stayed there longer . . . longer . . . longer . . . and then disappeared. I sent a follow-up.

> **Me:** Is everything ok?

My nerves increased at her hesitation, and I took a steadying breath to keep my mind from wandering down a dangerous path of "what if?"

"Is everything okay?"

I looked up, somewhat surprised at being asked the very thing I'd just texted Natalie. I cleared my throat as I remembered where I was. Work gave me tunnel vision: anything related to my company made the rest of the world disappear. But I wasn't at home. Or in my office. I needed to stay present. Kyle was leaning against the counter again eyeing me curiously, a stack of sandwiches beside him. So much for helping.

"Well, yes. That is, *I* am, but I have a big event this weekend. I was just reaching out to my assistant about it."

"You think she's screwing things up?"

"No!" I said hurriedly, immediately feeling defensive about Natalie. "She's quite capable. She *is* my assistant after all, I'm just not used to being removed like this, especially when it's such an important event. *And* it was all by surprise. Natalie has never handled one on her own."

"How long has she been with you?"

"Almost . . . " I thought for a moment. "Five years."

Kyle's eyebrows shot up. "Seems like you should be able to take a step back and she should be able to handle things by now then, no? . . .unless you're a terrible boss who hasn't taught her a thing."

I opened my mouth to respond defensively, but paused when I saw he was still smiling. Was everything a joke to this man? And yet . . . his comment made me wonder. *Was I* a good boss? Had I been teaching

Natalie? Did I give her chances for growth? More musings for another time. I looked down, grateful to finally have a response.

Natalie: Everything is fine

Everything was "fine." What did that even mean? I thought about lecturing her on her use of the word—it felt way too ambiguous—but decided the best response would be to actually get to her.

"So, Kyle . . . what do you think the chances are of me getting out of here soon?"

"Well, I can't really answer that. But you could come along to deliver these sandwiches and ask George. He'll have a better idea than I do right now."

"You just drove here though. Don't you know how the roads are? Also, your mom just said an alert was sent asking everyone to stay off them."

"Well first off, all I did was head up the driveway. "

"He's staying further back on the property," Mary said as she reentered the room, my folded clothes in hand. "And did I not just say there were reckless residents who wouldn't heed?"

"Oh! It's you!"

Kyle rolled his eyes. "Come on, mom, you know I have things to do to look out for the town, and you know one of the reasons why."

Mary let out a huff. "I suppose I do. Just be careful, please?"

"You know I will be," he said and gave her another kiss. "So what do you say we find out about those roads together?" He held up the bag he'd placed the sandwiches in. "We've got some hungry workers out there."

I looked down at my notebook, resigned myself to the fact there was nothing I could immediately do, as frustrated as that made me, and back up at Kyle.

"Sure," I said as I closed it and took my clothes from Mary. "Just let me put these on. Thank you for washing them, Mary."

"Well now, you don't have to change," Kyle said with a smirk. "My grandma's nightgown looks delightful on you."

"Oh, Kyle," Mary swatted him on the shoulder as I scurried out of the room.

Historically, cheek hue depended solely on makeup selection, but now I found myself shaking my head and wondering how this relative stranger had the ability to make me blush so dang much.

5

"I'm not sure those boots are gonna cut it," Kyle raised an eyebrow as I descended the stairs, back in my jeans and boots but a borrowed sweatshirt with a bright cardinal on a snowy bough in the center. Thankfully, Mary did in fact know how to care for cashmere and had hung my sweater to dry. My hair was still in a bun, just a bit less lopsided.

"These are the only boots I have with me. They'll do fine. After all, they're the same as yesterday, and I walked down the hill in them!"

I conveniently left out the part where I constantly slipped. It got to the point where I slid my feet along the street more than lifted them, and contemplated sitting down and actually sliding on more than one occasion, stopped only by the thought of a frozen, wet butt.

"It's a wonder you didn't fall! That's one bitch of a hill." He shrugged and opened the door, letting in a gust of wind and snow just like the night before.

I let out a little laugh—I was going for carefree—but realized he was right as soon as I stepped outside: the snow was deeper than my booties, and the inside began filling up after the first step.

"Oooookay, that's cold!" I all but yelped.

"Here: follow in my footsteps."

"I choose to blaze my own path," I said defiantly, but did as he instructed and stepped in the prints he left behind on the way to his truck—it helped. He pulled open the door and I went to climb in but paused with one foot on the runner as the connection hit me. "Wait . . . a bitch of a hill . . . is that why it's called Dog Hill?!?"

"Legend has it," he said with a grin before closing the door behind me. He'd started the truck while I'd gone to change, and I was grateful for the immediate warmth. "Do you mind if I plow the driveway as we go? I've already done a couple passes but I'd like to stay on top of it."

His phrasing didn't immediately make me think of winter weather, and I was appalled and surprised at the direction my mind went.

"N—no. Not at all. I'm at your mercy after all."

Kyle chuckled, lowered the plow and started to clear the driveway as we made our way to the road, and I couldn't help but shake the thought we were both secretly thinking of innuendos. A wandering mind was so unlike me . . .

With the driveway cleared, we left for the station and discovered the actual streets were in dire need of a plow as well. I could immediately tell my car would be rendered useless on the roads in their current state, and I let out a groan. Kyle, on the other hand, maneuvered his truck with skill, albeit at a slower pace than I imagined he drove on the regular. His wipers moved at a ferocious speed, trying futilely to keep the flakes away.

"These roads do *not* seem good. Are you sure it's okay to be out driving? And are you sure the crew's even out working??"

Kyle gave me a look that made me regret my choice of words for the clueless city-slicker they likely made me out to be. "Sorry. Right. Your mom explained a bit about all they have to do. Emergency access and all that."

"Right. And all that . . . " he went silent for a minute, and I wondered if I'd managed to annoy him. I glanced a peek at his expression, which looked more determined than annoyed. His jaw was clenched, and while I couldn't be sure which emotion was causing it, I could admit it did wonders for his profile. Damn he was handsome.

I felt the truck shift sideways slightly, and reached for the grab handle.

"It's alright," he said. "The roads are more slippery than I expected, but I can handle it."

I almost said 'oh I bet you can' but bit my tongue instead. Who even was I, right now? I thought about the last time Darren and I slept together and realized I couldn't quite remember when that was, which was embarrassing, frankly. I'd chalked it up to the two of us being busy. That was the case for me anyway, but I now knew it had to do with Darren getting a different type of busy: with another woman.

We pulled into the town garage located next to the fire station a minute later, and I hopped out of the truck with the sandwiches.

Kyle appeared beside me and we headed inside where a few men, including George, were holding cups of coffee and standing by a heater in one of the garage bays.

"Breakfast has arrived" Kyle said with a motion in my direction.

When the men chuckled, he quickly added, "Mary made sandwiches —Ms. Ev . . . I mean, Charity here helped."

Was he blushing? I grinned and held out the bag. "Gentlemen."

"Thanks so much Charity," George smiled as he took the goods. "Much appreciated. And nice to see you again—*not* out frozen in the snow somewhere."

"Any updates?" Kyle asked as he went to pour coffee from the metal carafe that sat on a counter to one side. "The roads are a rink—if only the temperature hadn't gone up the last couple of days. That bit of rain is a sheet of ice under all this snow." He turned to me. "Coffee? Lottie roasts it herself at the café."

I gave a nod, never one to turn down a second cup in the morning.

"Not much," George answered as he took a bite of one of the sandwiches. "We've been making our way through town non-stop, just trying to keep emergency access open. But it's falling at a steady rate, and that wind is making some giant drifts."

"And then, like you mentioned, that ice underneath it all isn't helping," added one of the others. "Poses a definite risk for snapping limbs and outages."

Kyle nodded solemnly. "Sugar? Cream?" He directed towards me.

"A splash of cream," I answered. He gave me a funny look—was it judgey??—but did as I asked and handed me the cup. "I haven't gotten any outage notifications as of yet," he said to the men standing. "Let's just hope it stays—"

As if on cue, the lights in the garage flickered and went out.

"Well shit," George muttered in the darkness.

A moment later, the rumble of an engine started and the lights came back on.

"Glad we made sure the generator was in working order."

"What happened?" I asked.

"Not sure," Kyle said as he pulled out his phone. "Come with me." He pressed the phone to his ear and I followed him back outside, pulling my coat tight to try and keep some of the wind and snow at bay. "Did you lose power?" He said as greeting to whomever he'd called as we got back in his truck. "It went out at the garage. I sent a text to Chief and they're on backup as well. Someone should check in with Lauren; did the community center get that damn generator fixed?"

Silence for a beat. "You know my concern if it's widespread. Could be a branch on a wire but—"

More silence, and I could just make out a voice rising on the other end of the line. "Grover, I'm not trying to overstep. But this isn't really the time to—" I looked sideways at Kyle. The muscle in his jaw twitched again. "What did you plan on doing, exactly? Right. . . . I'll take care of it."

This Kyle, it seemed, was quite the go-getter. I could appreciate that. He also wasn't the biggest fan of whomever he was speaking to. If we were still in the era of wall phones, I had the feeling he'd slam the receiver down. As it was, he tossed his phone on the dash with a disgusted sigh.

"Everything alright?"

"Yes—no. Well, I don't actually know. But I plan to find out. I need to stay in town to check on a few things. Should I bring you back to mom's? Or we could see if Lottie's or The Hearth has power and you could stay there for a bit. I noticed you brought your bag. I found myself wondering why on earth you'd bothered since we were just doing a drop-off, but now I see you'd had some foresight."

It was true—I *had* grabbed my things when we'd left with the sandwiches, but I was surprised he'd noticed. It reminded me just how little we knew about each other; most people would be surprised if I *wasn't* carrying my things around. "Downtime" was meant for working.

"I don't want to be a bother. If what you need to do is around here then I'll just stay nearby. Seems like you've got a lot to worry about."

"Somedays it feels like an entire town, actually" he said as he turned onto the road, carefully drove his truck up a ways, then pulled over again in front of a building with a sign that read "Lottie's" in pink letters just visible through the snow.

"Either she's still got power or the generator is doing its job, so it looks like you're good to go. I'll be back as soon as I can. Get a cinnamon bun—they're delicious."

Sitting around eating a pastry was certainly not how I thought I'd spend two days before the Hannigan wedding, but what could I do about it? Kyle seemed preoccupied with quite a bit at present, and I had a feeling my vehicle and a celebrity marriage were *not* high on the priority list.

I entered the café as he rumbled away behind me. Inside, I was met by a rush of warmth and an array of delicious scents. My eyes roamed the space and immediately settled on the word "adorable" as descriptor. The walls were blush-colored with a subtle floral design, and the floor boasted white hexagon tile with black rosettes. Gold light fixtures hung over a black-topped counter that featured a section for sitting, the register, and a display case for baked goods, with a garland covered in faux snow and twisted with white lights strung across the front. The place wasn't overly large, but fit a scattering of bistro-style tables. Each had a tiny ceramic Christmas tree in the middle in either white or pale pink. A jazz version of "Have Yourself A Merry Little Christmas" played quietly from hidden speakers.

A woman stepped out from the back and rushed over when she saw me.

"Oh! Good morning! I'm surprised to see someone out in all this! Take a seat wherever you'd like. As you can see, it's not the busiest this morning. The power went out a few minutes ago so thank goodness I had a generator installed. I'm in the middle of a batch of danish!"

I gave her a smile as I looked around the empty café, chose a seat in the back corner, and pulled out my laptop and notebooks.

"I've never seen your face around here before . . . ?" the woman continued as she approached.

She was around the same age as me, I guessed. Her hair was piled on top of her head in a chignon, and her blue eyes twinkled. She also appeared pregnant, but I'd learned never to remark on something like that until it was confirmed; I'd die on the spot if I said something and turned out to be wrong.

"No, I was traveling through last night when the snow caught me off guard."

"Ah!" She said, recognition flitting across her face. "You're the city girl, then."

"Oh? You've heard of me?"

"My husband Mike is one of the firefighters. He heard it from George over at public works. I'm Charlotte, but almost everyone calls me Lottie. Welcome to my café!"

She held out her hand and I shook it, even though I thought it a bit friendly for a customer greeting. But maybe that's how it went in a small town.

"Thanks! It's really lovely in here. And we were just at public works dropping off some breakfast, actually."

She beamed at the compliment. "I appreciate that. It took quite a while to get to this point. Plenty of people here would see the town disappear into oblivion before they welcomed change. My pink aesthetic was a hard sell. Thankfully I'm good friends with one of the councilmen who helped get just enough of the council and zoning board on my side to move forward. And who's 'we'?"

"This guy named Kyle. He dropped me off. He drives a white truck and seems to know quite a few people around town. Do you know him? I'm sure there are multiple K—"

"Oh I know Kyle, alright." She said with a smirk that had me wondering at the meaning.

"Oh! Great! Well, he's been a big help since I got here, and we made some sandwiches with his mom this morning."

"You've met his mom already? Wow."

"Oh. Oh! No, it's not like that," I laughed nervously. "He brought me to stay at his place, since there's no hotel or anything here." I could practically see her wheels turning as she mulled over all I was saying, and realized "he brought me to stay at his place" was adding more color to a particular type of picture. "His mom's place, that is. . . . while he went home. Anyway, he mentioned you roast your own coffee? I'd love a cup. Can you make it a latte? Oh. And a cinnamon bun if you have them?"

"One latte coming up. And a cinnamon bun, too! Good choice: they're Kyle's favorite." She bustled off, and I turned my attention— or the first time since this whole escapade had taken place—to the last message I'd received from Darren.

Darren: Can we talk about this?

6

I didn't necessarily *want* to talk, but I wasn't one to leave things unfinished, and I'd hung up on Darren mid-conversation yesterday. So I pressed call, and was unsurprised when he picked up after the third ring. He always said he considered that the right amount: he didn't want to appear too eager to any of his clients. It didn't matter that's not what I was, it was a habit that transferred to everyone.

"Evans," he said by way of greeting. "Finally."

"Finally?"

"Yes. Your hang-ups usually result in a callback a few minutes later. This was . . . quite a bit longer. Although maybe I deserved it."

"You think?" It was true—hanging up in exasperation was something I'd done on more than one occasion. I wasn't thrilled to admit it, but like he said, I usually called again. "There was a situation that kept me from calling back."

And how was I supposed to feel learning he always expected me to call again? Now I wondered if he'd have reached out instead if I let the silence linger. Had I been the one to keep this going longer than it was ever meant to?

"Look, I know the timing was shit."

"I'd say. I thought January was supposed to be the month for breaking up?"

He laughed his nervous laugh, and I knew he was running fingers through his mop of sandy hair. "A couple weeks before Christmas also tends to be popular . . . "

Once a statistician, always a statistician, and honestly, that was one of the reasons I thought we worked. Darren was steady. He was logical. He wasn't known for extremes. There was comfort in that; a sense of certainty. I liked his predictability, although breaking up with me so he could bring another woman home for the holidays didn't exactly fall under that category.

"So, just to be clear . . . " I don't know why I wanted to know. It wasn't like it changed anything. "You were cheating on me?"

"NO!" was his rushed response. "That is . . . I guess it depends on your definition. There's been a lot of talking. We've had coffee together a few times. There's definitely attraction. And that's when I knew you and I were . . . " there was silence for a moment. "Well, I told her it couldn't move forward until I ended things with you."

Ended. Such permanence there. I wanted to be mad at him, I really did. But the anger I'd felt when I was spinning on ice had all but dissipated. In fact, I was surprised how little I'd thought of him since he broke the news yesterday, and how easily I'd been distracted not only by my predicament but the man who was helping me. What *did* I feel? There was disappointment, sure. After all, this was not in my plans. Darren had been the checkmark next to "significant other" on my list of life goals for the past seven years. But I was also feeling . . . dare I say relieved? He really *was* a nice guy, but this whole thing was so unexpected it felt entirely un-Darren-like. Which meant: 1. I didn't know him as well as I thought, and 2. perhaps he wasn't the right guy to check that box, after all.

Lottie returned with my latte and placed it in front of me with a sympathetic smile and a plate bearing not one but two cinnamon rolls. A blush crept up my cheeks as I realized she probably knew what was going on since the place was empty aside from me. I was certain she could hear my conversation and was piecing things together. If she thought I was about to cry though, she'd be mistaken.

I gave her a mega-watt smile to prove it and mouthed a 'thank you.'

"I have to say Darren, I'm a little surprised. This whole thing feels so out of character. Is everything okay with you?"

" . . . you . . . I'm ending our relationship, and you're asking how *I'm* doing?"

I shrugged, even though he couldn't see it. "I guess I am. We've been together for years Darren. I can't just suddenly *not* worry about your welfare."

"Wow. I mean, yeah. I suppose you're right. And I'm good Chair. I'm really good. She just . . . I don't know. She brings out this side of me I didn't even know I had. She makes me want to try new things. Be a bit spontaneous!"

"I'm sorry, what?! YOU?? Darren James McElney? SPONTANEOUS?"

"Don't faint. I said 'a bit.' Baby steps. I tried sushi the other day."

"I honestly don't know what to say. Did you like it??" Darren never tried *anything* new.

"Absolutely not."

I laughed. Now *that* was a Darren-like response. We were both silent for a moment, each presumably lost in thought. I, for one, was thinking how very friendly this conversation was. It was typical for us. I'd always thought that was a good sign: lasting relationships were built on friendship, were they not? But maybe I'd been trying to force us into a romantic box we didn't fit in. Which was perhaps good enough for me, but clearly not Darren.

"So . . . what's her name?"

"Amy."

"And you're bringing her home? Since when do you go home for the holidays?"

"Well, I did before we got together. Working through the holidays was sort of your thing, Charity. I just went along with it."

"That's a big thing to give up."

"Yeah, well, you make a convincing case . . . "

"Hmm. That's true."

"She lights me up inside, Chair. We had a good run but . . . "

"You want to be lit up."

"Yeah. That."

I opened my mouth to tell him the dangers of all that: being lit up meant the risk of being engulfed. Turned to ash. Loving someone fiercely opened up the possibility of a heart being torn apart just as fierce if they were to leave. Or worse.

"I want that for you, too, Charity."

"I'm not sure I'm the type."

"Oh I think you are, I just think I'm not the guy."

I looked up at the sound of the café door opening to find Kyle walking in. His eyes settled on me as he brushed snow off his jacket, and he gave a smile that made my stomach flip nervously. He made his way over and sat in the chair opposite me.

I cleared my throat. "Well Darren, I've got to get going."

"Yeah. Me too. Thanks for calling me back Charity. And thanks for being so good about all this. You're exceptional."

"Thanks Darren. Goodbye."

"Bye, Charity."

I fixed Kyle with a smile.

"Cinnamon bun?" I asked by way of greeting. "Lottie gave me two."

"Gladly," he said as he picked up the gooey goodness and took a bite. "Mm. So good! You gonna eat yours or what?"

I picked up my own and bit into it to discover he wasn't lying: it *was* good. The right balance of cinnamon and sugar. Perfectly baked. Gooey, and covered in the right amount of icing.

"Oh wow. This is delicious," I gushed and took another bite that earned an appreciative nod in response.

"Hey Lottie," Kyle hollered toward the kitchen, startling me. "You've got another cinnamon bun fan!"

A whoop sounded from the back.

"And how about that coffee? What did you get?"

I picked up my drink and took a sip. "A latte. And oh! This is really good too!"

His eyes widened. "Of course it is. But a plain old latte??"

"Yes? Is that a problem?"

"It IS actually."

I looked at my cup. "Are you going to tell me I'm being pretentious for ordering a latte in a small-town café and I should have settled for drinking it black or with milk and sugar?" I scowled at him, ready to defend my latte to the death.

"Easy there, I wasn't going to say all that. The opposite, in fact. You only had cream earlier, and now, a latte. Normally I'd say that was a solid choice to really taste how great her fresh-roasted coffee is. But Christmas is less than a week away! The only acceptable beverages have to include peppermint, chocolate, sprinkles—*something* to make them festive!"

"I . . . oh. What?"

"You heard me. Do you dislike any of the things I mentioned?"

"No, I just don't—"

"'Really get into the season.' I remember. And it's a tragedy. Allow me, please."

I wasn't sure what I was about to "allow" but I found myself nodding.

"Lottie!" he hollered again, and she appeared from the back room.

"You're lucky it's you. Anyone else called for me that way and I'd slap 'em upside the head."

Kyle smirked. "It's because she married my best friend."

Lottie rolled her eyes. "Actually it's because he's a councilman and I don't want any business violations suddenly cropping up."

"Wait . . . " I turned from Lottie to Kyle, unable to hide the surprise on my face. "You're a councilman? Ohhh, the one who helped get your renovations through?"

Lottie nodded in affirmation, while Kyle leaned back and crossed his arms in front of his chest, which somehow made him look impossibly cute. "Indeed I am a councilman. And indeed I am 'the one' who helped bring this pink pastry palace to fruition. Does that surprise you?"

"No, I . . . That is . . . " I took a deep breath. This man kept making me forget my words. It was very unlike me. I was a professional for goodness sake! I took life serious. And yet, I found myself wanting to joke with him. "Don't you have to be old to be on a town council? Or did you suffer head trauma and now you *think* you're a council member and the town loves you so much they go along with it?"

Lottie snorted out a laugh, and Kyle narrowed his eyes. "Lottie, get this woman a Snow Day, would you? She needs some sweetening up. One for me too, of course. And as for you, Ms. Evans . . . "

"I told you—"

"Oh no, this deserves formalities. I'll have you know, *Ms. Evans*, I've been an *elected*—not pretend—councilman in the fine town of Auburn Falls for the last seven years. I'm in the middle of my second term." He puffed out his chest proudly and I laughed at the sight.

"I didn't mean to offend you *councilman*, I just assumed you were too young to hold such a position."

"Well, to be fair, I was the youngest elected member in the history of the town. But also we need younger people to get involved! No offense meant to those who have given decades of their lives to civic service, of course, but we need a balance if we're to see towns move forward in any sensible manner. Get stuck in the past and get left behind."

"Was that your campaign slogan?"

"Perhaps . . . " he took another bite of his cinnamon bun and I couldn't help but stare as he licked a wayward bit of frosting off his lip.

I looked away. "Funny, I've got one of those titles too."

"Council member?"

"No, no—youngest something."

Lottie brought our drinks over and we paused to take a sip. A Snow Day turned out to be a delightful concoction of peppermint and chocolate, but it was lighter than I expected, and despite being a hot beverage, it felt cool and refreshing thanks to the peppermint. I couldn't help but think of . . .

"It's like a snow day, right!?"

"That's exactly what I was thinking actually. It's really good! Aptly named."

"It's peppermint and white chocolate blended with espresso. My favorite."

"Wow, it may be mine now too."

Kyle looked smug, and I found myself laughing at the expression.

"Don't look proud of yourself or anything," I rolled my eyes.

"Oh, I will. This is much more festive than a plain ol' latte." He raised his cup toward me and took another sip. "Well, as enjoyable as this little reprieve has been, we should probably get back home. The snow is expected to keep up until evening at least."

At his words, the reality of our present situation hit me again: I looked out the window at the world of white.

"Oh, wow. Right. Of course. Did you figure out what made the power go out?"

"A branch on some wires. I reported it to the power company but they won't be out to fix it until after the weather clears. And then, of course, it will depend how many other places lose power before this is over. Could be a few days."

I nodded in silent understanding as we stood, but my mind was reeling. What did this mean for my car? And getting to the manor?

Kyle put money on the table and called out for Lottie.

"We're off, Lottie. I'd close up and head home if I were you. No sense wasting the gas. I have a feeling Charity and I might be your only customers today."

"I agree, I just want to finish up a batch of pizza pinwheels for the crew before Mike drops me home."

"Always looking out," Kyle said fondly. "Just be sure to take care of yourself, too. And that little one you're carrying around."

Ah. Confirmation of pregnancy! Kyle held the door for me.

"Always playing the part of the brother I never had," Lottie said warmly. "Come see me again once the snow stops," she directed at me as she waved from her place behind the counter, one hand resting on her stomach.

I smiled and nodded, which I figured was better than turning her down outright—after all, if I could only wrangle my life back on track,

I'd be out of Auburn Falls sooner rather than later, with no chance to pop back for a visit.

39

7

"I figured we'd make a quick pitstop," Kyle said as we settled in his truck again and he pulled onto the snowy road.

"Where to?"

"A snow bank."

"Huh?"

In answer he skillfully—albeit slowly—maneuvered the truck back through town and up the hill I'd walked down the night before. As I noticed how narrow the road actually was, without much clearance on either side, I offered up a silent prayer of thanks the street wasn't a busy one. Considering how dark and wintry it'd been last night, it would have been near impossible for me to have avoided being hit.

"Where's Jackie?"

"You named your car." Kyle said, in a tone of appreciation.

"Of course I did. My dad was a car guy. He said they responded better when you named them. His name was Jack, so . . . Does your truck have a name?"

"Of course she does. This is Dorothy."

He pulled Dorothy over—as much as he could without sending it down the same ditch I'd put my precious BMW in—and we hopped out. I looked around and noticed a mound a few hundred feet up that seemed slightly out of place at the same time as Kyle.

"There she is."

"We're not . . . are you going to try to get her out right now?"

Kyle grabbed a couple of brushes from his truck. "Unfortunately no, that'll have to wait for a proper tow truck and the weather to break. Not that Dorothy couldn't handle it of course."

"Right right," I said with a smirk, trying to hide my disappointment at having to leave my car there longer, but understanding the situation. "So what *are* we doing exactly?"

"Well, we might as well get the rest of your things."

"Oh." Getting the rest of my belongings made sense, of course, but it also made my delay in town feel a bit more indefinite. Not exactly something I wanted.

"Unless you'd rather not? I just thought you might like a shower and some new clothes. If the snow lets up this evening, Paul might be able to get the car out. Of course, it'll take the night for the streets to be plowed beyond the pass for emergency access, but maybe you'll feel up for trying your hand on the snowy roads again and hope for the best?"

I shook my head. "Not if I can help it. One ice skating performance in a two ton vehicle is more than enough for me."

"Smart choice. And I have to say, as a member of our town council, I'd feel personally responsible if anything happened to you within our borders, knowing I could have prevented it if you'd just hung back awhile. So what do you say? Shower and a change of clothes?" He held one of the brushes out to me.

"I say I really want to get to the manor, but it sounds like I don't have much of a choice at present." I took the brush. "And hey, what are you trying to say anyway? That I smell?"

That charming chuckle rang out again as he began clearing snow from my car's trunk.

"Not at all, you do disheveled delightfully. Just want you to be comfortable. Although . . . " he paused mid-brush. "You *did* look adorable in that nightgown, so maybe we should leave it all here after all. If you have to be tortured by staying another night, you should wear that again."

"While it's true I'm supposed to be at the manor, I'd hardly call this torture. And you leave that nightgown out of this!" I dropped the brush, picked up some snow, bunched it into a ball and tossed it in Kyle's direction. He ducked, I missed, and instantly regretted grabbing it with my bare hands.

"Okay, that's cold" I said, shaking them and reaching down to retrieve the brush.

"Yeah. It's *snow*. And serves you right. After all, I was just trying to pay you a compliment."

I shook my head and focused on brushing the rest of the snow aside, but it hit me then—more direct than my poorly aimed snowball—that we were flirting. When had I last flirted with someone? Did I *ever* flirt? Darren and I were practical from the start. Seven years of practical. We wove our lives together in a way that was convenient—that made sense. Our relationship felt like a well-known dance: everything fit together. Our work ethic, our mid-day coffee meets, our weekly date night which automatically populated in our synced calendar . . . Although the reminder was rather superfluous since the details didn't change: Thursday. 7 p.m. Giancarlo's. Veal parm for Darren. Salad and risotto for me.

But did we ever *flirt?* I didn't think so. I didn't think either of us needed it, and I took comfort in the lukewarm, consistent existence that was our relationship. Yet now, here I was, single a day and flirting with someone else.

"And he tried sushi for fuck's sake!"

"I'm sorry . . . what?"

Kyle's voice startled me out of the rabbit hole I'd fallen down and made me realize I'd said that last bit aloud. I jumped, lost my footing in the process, and in the next instant I was letting out a shriek and being pulled down by gravity. I saw Kyle lunge for me in my peripheral, but he wasn't quite quick enough. I scrambled to grab onto something to steady myself and settled on an overhead branch, but it proved too flimsy.

I landed in the snow with a *thump*, taking a pile down on top of me thanks to my choice of tree arm, that was followed with a crunching sound. The latter confused me at first, until a wetness started seeping through my pants that told me this wasn't just a ditch, but a frozen stream.

Silence hung in the air for just a moment while I sat, somewhat stunned—and, alright, slightly embarrassed—covered in snow with wet pants. And then Kyle's composure broke, and his deep laugh filled the snowy air. I wanted to be annoyed at him for his reaction, but realized I was anything but, and I felt the corners of my mouth tug upward. It wasn't the first time this had happened since I'd met Councilman Kyle, and the lack of control I had over my reactions around him left me feeling frustrated, a bit fluttery, and nervous in a good way.

I stayed silent but reached into my pocket, pushed a button on my key fob, and Jackie's trunk popped opened.

8

The hot water felt divine. After sitting in snow and icy water, I wasn't quite able to warm up again, even after Kyle helped me up, brushed snow off my back and shoulders, and hurried me into the truck. He'd turned the heat on blast while I chattered like a fool, then returned to my car to gather my things.

Perhaps he sensed my frustration-embarrassment soup, because he stayed silent for the ride back to his mom's. Anytime I glanced at him I swore his lips were twitching, but he didn't make fun of me for falling, and I was grateful for the quiet. I wasn't sure how I'd respond to any joking just then. Would I laugh along with him? Or be annoyed I was so clearly *not* in control? It was something else I found alarming, since I prided myself on always knowing just what to say or do.

"I'll bring your things upstairs," Kyle said when we pulled in. "Go on in and take a shower."

He didn't need to tell me twice. I hurried inside, but not before noticing how lovely the house was now that I was seeing it during the day. It was solid brick, with black shutters and frosted windows; a warm glow emanated from within thanks to candles in the middle of each window that added a bit of brightness to the muted colors of a stormy day. A pine wreath with a velvet bow hung on the front door beneath a fanned-glass window.

I pushed inside, took off my sopping boots—that's what I got for not wearing something waterproof and practical like Kyle suggested—and scurried upstairs to the bathroom.

Now, thoroughly warmed, clean, and smelling divine thanks to the vanilla almond toiletries the shower held, I stepped out and returned to the bedroom to find Kyle had in fact brought up all my things.

Knowing he'd been so close to me while I was in the shower, if only for a moment, led to another rush of warmth that had nothing to do with hot water. I shook my head; I was being ridiculous. Dangerously so.

"Be practical, Charity." I muttered to myself as I dressed. I needed to do something level-headed. I needed to make a list. I ran a brush through my hair, applied light makeup so I wouldn't earn the 'delightfully disheveled' title forever, and went downstairs with my laptop and notebook.

I wandered through the living room and back to the kitchen where I found Kyle and Mary sitting at a table in the breakfast nook, framed by bay windows looking out on the snowy scene, mugs clasped in their hands.

I paused in the doorway, ready to retreat instead of interrupt their time together, when they looked my way as though they sensed my presence.

"Sorry—I didn't mean to interrupt."

Mary gave me a giant smile that matched Kyle's. I guess I knew where he got it. I realized then there hadn't been any mention of his father, but our relationship was too new for me to inquire.

Relationship. Hah! Could I even call it that? Our 'brief interlude' would be more appropriate considering my impending departure. I chose to ignore the fact I had no clue when exactly that might be as of yet. And why did the thought of leaving cause a slight pang? My events were my life! *Nothing* was more important. Certainly not a stopover in a random small town with a pleasant group of people.

"Oh, no, not at all!" Mary said. "Kyle and I were just taking a moment to enjoy."

I made my way further into the room. "Er . . . enjoy what?"

"Just . . . enjoy. The moment. Would you like to join us?" She gestured to the chair beside her.

People actually enjoyed just sitting around? That was so *not* my cup of whatever they were drinking. I was about to say so: the words "I like to use the minutes I'm given on productivity, thanks" loaded on my tongue, but then I saw Kyle lean back, much like he had at the café, and raise an eyebrow like he was waiting to see what I'd do. It felt like a challenge.

"Uh, sure. Yes. Alright . . . " I put my things on the island and took a seat. Kyle's expression remained—amusement mixed with interest?— as I sat for a moment. I tried to picture myself from his perspective: back straight, hands clasped on my lap. I probably seemed so freaken uptight. I took a deep breath and tried to relax, but found myself squirming under Kyle's gaze. It broke a moment later when there was a *thunk* followed by an "ow!"

"What was that for??" he asked his mother.

"Stop staring at our guest and get her some cocoa."

He shook his head but rose, and returned a minute later with my own steaming mug topped with a heap of whipped cream and sprinkles.

"Oh wow, this is quite the cup."

"It's the only way to do cocoa. We don't do things halfway around here," he said as he sat again.

"I can see that . . . "

I took a sip, and as the delicious sweetness slid down my throat—followed with the unexpected and delightful taste of cinnamon—my eyes returned to the window and the scene outside. The snow let up slightly, I realized. Enough for more of the outside to be noticeable, like the trees that bordered the property. Most were bare, of course, but conifers were scattered throughout, their green adding a pop of color. Snow in the city could create lovely scenes, but out here . . . this was different. It felt like I'd hopped into one of the Christmas cards I received, despite never sending any out myself. As if in answer, and to cement that point, a flash of red flew in front of my line of sight, then came to stop toward the right. It registered a moment later: a cardinal. And now, seeing one contrasted against the white of winter, I realized I wasn't sure how long it'd been since I'd last seen one in person. The last time I was at my childhood home, maybe? Before everything changed. I took a deep breath and felt my muscles relax in a way that startled me.

I gave a little shake of my head and drew my focus away from the pine trees, away from the snow and the vibrant bird, and back into the kitchen to find both my companions staring at me.

"What did you put in this cup??"

The single-dimple smirk. "Just love . . . "

At the word, my muscles coiled right back up.

"Which we put into everything we make, and serve with a bit of ambiance." Kyle finished, waving his hand toward the window.

"Well I . . . actually I'm not sure the last time I took a minute to just sit." I was leaning forward now, my forearms resting on the table, cradling my mug the same way they'd been. "I think I could get used to this."

I looked around the table and knew I meant more than just sitting with a pretty scene—the company was good too. It was a thought that had me shoving back the chair and standing.

"Which is exactly why I don't do it more often. Too much to do to get used to lallygagging."

I picked up my cup and backed my way over to the island. Kyle's eyebrows shot up, and he quietly repeated "lallygagging" like it was the strangest word in the world and, honestly, I wasn't sure what made me say it. Lallygagging. Mirth. Sitting around. Cups of cocoa with whipped cream and sprinkles. This place was getting to me, and I wasn't sure it was in a good way.

"If it's alright I'm just going to camp out here and do some work."

"Of course," Mary said, rising herself, "I want to get dinner started anyway. I'm assuming we can expect you to join us? I'm making lasagna, and some fresh bread with the dough I set to rise earlier. Nothing like a nice hearty meal on a cold winter's day. If I feel up for it, I may add a dessert. My daughter would usually join us but I'm not sure she'll make it today. Not unless Kyle feels like a pick up . . . "

"If she'd been ready when we were down there this morning she'd be here already. " Kyle said as he brought their mugs to the sink. "Not my fault she sleeps in so late. And didn't you tell me earlier you'd rather I stay off the roads? I'll get her if you really want me too ma, but I'd rather take a break until this clears. I've already been all over the place taking care of what should honestly be Grover's responsibilities."

"I know dear, I know." She gave him a comforting pat on the shoulder. "And it's alright. Emmeline is sure to give you quite the guilt trip about it, but she'll be fine."

"I've been going on those 'trips' my entire life. I'm immune. But I'll bring her some leftovers tomorrow. Now, about *you* Charity . . . "

I shot him a questioning look when he turned back around, hoping . . . hoping what? That he'd say my car was out of the ditch and I could head to the manor? Or that he'd say it was still good and stuck and I'd get to enjoy dinner with the two of them and another night in a flannel nightgown and cozy bed? While I waited for his answer, for the first time in a long while, thanks to thoughts of home cooked meals and actual homey homes and cardinal sightings, I found myself wanting to call my mom. It'd been a while. I flipped open my notebook and grabbed the pink pen I reserved for personal tasks that were honestly few and far between: call Laura.

"All things considered, you'll definitely have to spend another night." Kyle explained. "George didn't say much when we were down there to suggest the roads would be cleared any sooner, especially with the snow still coming. And Paul said at this point getting your car free should wait until it clears, too. I know that must be disappointing. I know you said you had an event to get to."

I was confused; the emotion I felt at the confirmation I'd be staying longer was decidedly *not* disappointment. In fact, it felt unexpectedly like glee, but it was fighting with a bit of panic at not having the reins at the Hannigan wedding. I took a deep breath to take control of my feelings. Kyle noticed.

"Are you okay? Is your boss going to give you a hard time? What kind of a person are they, anyway? It's not like this is a little flurry."

I laughed, "Er . . . well actually my boss is a severe workaholic and it's safe to say they like to be front and center at any and all events related to the company. She's been that way since its inception. Less room for error." I paused a moment for dramatic affect. "And *she* is also me."

"Oh!" Mary turned from the counter where she was slicing squash for the lasagna. "You have your own event company! How marvelous! You must be so proud and—wait . . . you said your event this weekend is at Juniper Manor?"

I nodded, feeling pride rise up as I had an inkling I knew where this was headed.

"Kyle! My goodness do you know what this means?!"

"Uh . . . no?" he admitted, looking less than pleased at being in the dark.

"It means we have the event planner for the Hannigan wedding in our home! Sarabeth Hannigan is getting married there this weekend!"

"Oh no," Kyle rolled his eyes. "I hope you're ready for 100 questions from mom. She's obsessed with the Hannigan family. So is Emma."

Mary looked affronted. "I am not!" But at Kyle's pointed look, she changed her tune. "Well, alright. Maybe a little. I just find them fascinating! They're the closest we've got to royalty! Especially since their grandmother was an actual *princess*!"

"Be that as it may, the rest of them don't have any titles since she decided to marry an American non-royal. The rest of them are just American citizens like the rest of us."

"Excuse me young man, but they're not exactly like the rest of us— not with the kind of money they have!"

I looked back and forth between them, amused at their easy banter.

Mary turned her attention back to me. "You must have spent a lot of time with them. You have to tell me all about it! And oh, how wonderful for your company!"

This was the most animated I'd seen Mary since we met. She was waving her knife around as she spoke, until Kyle went over and gently took it from her hand.

"Should I finish this?"

She nodded in answer and joined me at the island. I glanced briefly at my notebook then shut it again—once more without any progress. I truly couldn't remember when I'd gone so long without making several lists and checking them off. It was jarring. It was unsettling. It was . . . admittedly less stressful.

9

Kyle had not been exaggerating.

Twenty minutes later Mary knew all the details about the upcoming wedding, and while her interest was due to the participants, I enjoyed answering her questions since ultimately they had more to do with my planning than the Hannigans. When it came to answering more personal questions, for the most part I was useless.

"I've been keeping up on all the news about them; Emmeline and I contemplated going to Juniper to try and get a glimpse of everything—"

"Or try to sneak in," Kyle muttered, earning an eye roll in response.

"But of course, the weather . . . "

Ah yes. The weather. "It got in the way of both our plans then, didn't it?"

"Indeed, although I still maintain my 'everything happens for a reason' stance. After all, it led to you being in my kitchen, talking about the Hannigans, didn't it?"

"Hmmm," I mused as I took a final sip of my second cup of cocoa. "What about death?"

"What about it?" Mary fixed me with an intense stare from across the island, seemingly unperturbed by my sudden switch in topic. And to be honest, I had no idea what made me ask such a question. The ease of conversation I felt with her had me opening up in ways that were entirely uncharacteristic.

"Do you maintain that view in relation to death? Especially unexpected or tragic death?" I said the words while simultaneously wondering what on earth I was doing—it was like my usual filter disappeared with my car beneath the snow. Serious subjects such as

49

this involved too much emotion. And political conversations? Forget it. I chose to keep my views close to my chest and politely went mute when any discussions cropped up, though I tried to keep them from happening in general. As event planner, I attempted to keep moods light and fun. I tried to walk back my question with a laugh and diverted back to the Hannigans.

"So what else would you like to know? That Sarabeth didn't actually want to get married at the manor? The decision was all her mo—"

"Now now, just a moment. You can't ask a question like that and then move along. I'd like to answer it."

"Oh. You would. Okay."

"I would. Now, I can't answer this without telling you I'm a woman of faith. Well, perhaps spiritual is a more applicable term. There's so many different words for things these days, I can hardly keep up. All I know is I believe this beautiful world has a Creator's hand behind it, and that same hand guides and comforts us. Now, for some, going through life without the belief in anything more is enough. Take all you see at face value and mosey through your days until it's done. And I don't bear any of them ill will as we're all on our own journey, and it's not my place to mind the path someone else is on. But for me . . . " Mary paused and gazed back outside. "Well, for me, I've always needed to believe in something more than life as a series of events. And because of that, I believe everything does happen for a reason, even if in the moment—or a long time after a moment—you don't know what that reason is. You see, I don't believe we're meant to always know. Sometimes, we're just meant to trust. And as in the case of a tragic or untimely death, well . . . the reason may very well be it was their time. Just like we're each on our own path during this life, I believe we're each on our own journey after it. Only the Creator and the individual knows what that journey looks like. Of course, I understand in the midst of your grief that's not something you want to hear. When my husband died, I think I would have slapped anyone who dared say something along the lines of 'it was his time' to me."

"Not likely, ma" Kyle piped up. I looked to find him leaning against the counter, listening. This answered my unasked question about his father then; turned out we were both down a parent.

I reached over—quite unexpectedly since historically I wouldn't say I considered myself all that affectionate—and placed my hand on Mary's. She put her other one on top, sandwiching mine. I didn't feel like opening up about my own dad just then, but I felt a silent sense of solidarity in the knowledge we'd both lost someone close to us.

"Well you never know," she smiled and shrugged. "But the point is, when you believe there's something more after this, when every fiber of your being knows that's true and the 'after' is more beautiful than anything you could find on this earthly plane, well . . . it acts as a balm. The upset over their death is because we're inherently selfish, you see. We're mad *we* can no longer see them. We're sad *we* can no longer touch them. We're the ones who can experience frustration because they were 'taken' from us. Our life no longer has them in it, and that can lead to an agony so intense it's breath-stealing. But like I said, we're all on our own path. We just get to walk along together for a while. And the ones who have already gone? Well . . . They're alright. I believe that. It's the ones left behind who have to learn how to keep on keepin' on, and some days that can be downright awful. But most days, having the belief in all I just mentioned, it keeps me going. It keeps me simultaneously humbled and in awe. So . . . yes. I still maintain it's all for a reason."

I looked down at my empty cup. My eyes had watered when Mary said "they're alright," and a tear formed unexpectedly and too quick for me to stop it like I usually did. I pulled my hand from Mary's, opened my notebook and tried to look busy scribbling some relative nonsense while keeping my face hidden. The tear dropped and left a wet circle on the paper, spreading the ink from the words behind it. This conversation was making me feel things I wasn't sure I wanted to feel. And with practical strangers! Yet I found myself asking a follow-up.

"What if you're wrong? What if life *is* just a series of events, and when you die, you're done? Lights out."

"I didn't always have this faith. I was raised in the church but, as it often happens, I lost my way for a time. But one day I was wandering a tag sale with a dear friend of mine . . . " Mary stood and walked out of the kitchen.

I was confused by the departure mid-sentence, but in her absence, I dared glance at Kyle. His back was turned as he pulled spices from the cabinet, and I took a moment to admire the way his dark jeans fit in all the right places, and how cozy—and sexy—his burgundy sweater looked. He turned around, and I averted my eyes, but not quite quick enough.

"Are you okay?" He asked, trying to hide a smile. "My mom has a way of making people feel things."

I nodded. Clearly this place was not safe for me. I'd worked hard—for years—to rein in my emotions, and not only because of my dad's death. I knew if I wanted to succeed as a female business owner I needed a can-do attitude and control over my feels that told others I was in command of everything—including my emotions. I couldn't sit around getting all blubbery.

"I'm just anxious to get back to work that's all" a slight lie, but sometimes that was needed to save face, and anyone who said they'd never done that was . . . well . . . probably lying. Most people don't actually want someone to lose it in front of them, anyway; they want people who keep it together. "My work is my life," I added.

Kyle opened his mouth to speak, and I had a feeling it would be a comment on work-life balance or something, but Mary returned with a frame in hand. She gave it to me and I looked down at what turned out to be embroidery. Delicate flowers encircled a quote that read:

> I would rather live my life as though there is a God, and die to find there isn't, then live as though there is no God, and die to find that there is.

"There's some debate on who actually said it, but that doesn't matter to me. Finding this," she said, "it brought me back. We were in this dusty, cluttered old mill used as a permanent home for a giant, weekly tag sale. I hadn't had much luck finding anything because there was simply too much. But I felt compelled to search through a stack of framed prints and found this." Mary ran her fingers over the glass. "When I read it, I felt my heart expand. This wasn't too long after my husband's death, and my heart was still so heavy I was constantly surprised I could stand with the weight. I stared for a good five minutes before my friend asked if I was okay. Truth was, I was more than okay. It felt like a puzzle piece slipped into place, and I knew that was how I wanted to live going forward. So to answer your question: maybe I am wrong. And if I am and when I die, that *is* it . . . well, then I won't care that I was wrong, will I? But believing otherwise gives me a peace and comfort that helps me every day of my life."

I didn't know how to respond, because I felt like *I* was in that tag sale, surrounded by too much to unpack. These were things I never let myself contemplate. The weight I'd felt since losing my dad was a weight I never considered might lift. My answer was to focus so intently on other things I forgot it existed.

Silence hung in the air for a moment, broken by Mary. "Well! That conversation took a turn. From the Hannigans to the Holy Spirit! I need to work on lunch!"

She rose and went to stand beside Kyle.

"Don't worry, mom. I've got it covered."

"Yes, I can see that. In that case I'll set the coffee brewing and get to work on the bread. And Charity, if you've got work to get to don't mind us. Although, if you'd like to regal me with more tales of the Hannigans I wouldn't mind that either. Just be ready for a repeat once Emmaline finds out."

"We're never gonna hear the end of it now that she knows you know them," Kyle said with an eye roll, which earned him a playful swat on the shoulder.

"I don't mind. It's a pretty big deal, and I'm definitely proud they chose us. My business was already successful in the greater Boston area, but this will undoubtedly propel the company even more. That is . . . " I took another look out the window and let out a groan, reality hitting me. "Assuming it actually goes off without a hitch . . ." My anxiety started to rise again, so I took a steadying breath. "I should be there," I all but whined. I pulled open the wedding notebook and starting pouring over the rest of the day's events and all that was supposed to be done.

Kyle's phone rang, and he looked at the screen then stepped out of the room as he answered.

"Who's taking care of everything since you're not there?"

"My assistant Natalie headed up the day before me, thank goodness, so she missed the storm. She's been handling it all."

Mary set a mini charcuterie in front of me I hadn't realized she'd been putting together. "I thought you were making bread!"

"I am, but I wanted to make sure you had something to eat while lunch finishes up."

"This is amazing." It wasn't just a board with crackers and cheese slices: she'd added sausages and deli slices, pretzels, a variety of nuts, several festive candies, small ramekins of dip . . . "This is fit for a party!"

"Oh well that bodes well. I'll be making a much larger version for the town's Christmas party."

"There's a Christmas party here?"

"Mmhmm! Christmas Eve." Mary grabbed a selection from the platter and looked at me with an excited twinkle in her eyes. "It's an annual event. The entire town looks forward to it. Although I'm not entirely sure how it will turn out this year; the woman who spearheaded most of the planning in recent years is in the last trimester with twins and has been on bedrest."

I half expected Mary to outright ask if I'd help with the planning despite the fact I'd hopefully be gone before then. I certainly *needed* to be gone. But she remained silent, enjoyed her bite from the charcuterie, washed her hands, and returned to shaping her bread dough.

Kyle came back and gave me a quick look before he averted his eyes and focused on the coffee machine. "Do you want one? I have some whiskey if you'd like it Irish . . ."

"Are you having one?"

He nodded, but didn't turn around. Instead he busied himself pouring the liquid into three mugs, and while I continued to secretly enjoy his backside, something seemed . . . off.

"What is it? Should I be worried you're offering me whiskey this early in the day?"

He turned around slowly. "I mean, it's after noon, so . . . How's your assistant doing at the manor?"

"She said everything was fine this morning." I wasn't a fan of his tone. It didn't feel cajoling, which seemed to be his M.O. with me. Instead it seemed . . . gentle. I suddenly felt lightheaded. What if she'd been appeasing me like I originally suspected?

"Do you know something I don't? Did something happen at the manor?"

He cleared his throat. "Um, well no, not exactly. How long did you tell her it'd be until you got there?"

"I mean, I didn't really specify. I just said 'hopefully soon.'"

He nodded solemnly. "You might want to call her and tell her it's going to be a day or two . . . "

10

"A day or TWO?? Two means the day of the wedding! Absolutely not." I shook my head in refusal. "What's going on?"

"That was George on the phone."

Kyle was quiet for a beat, which caused Mary and I to exclaim simultaneously, "Just say it!"

If the current situation wasn't making me so nervous, I probably would have laughed at our synchronicity.

"A tree came down. Across the road to the manor."

"THE road? Surely there's more than one way to get there."

He shook his head. "They don't advertise it as 'secluded grandeur' for nothing."

I gulped. "How did George find out?"

"He's often in contact with employees from area towns, especially during severe events like this. That communication is usually something a town manager handles but . . . "

Kyle and Mary gave each other a knowing look.

"Crap. I should be checking in more. There's a wedding hashtag we started using almost as soon as the engagement was announced to help with publicity, but it's like reading reviews. I've been scared to look. I wonder if it's impacted anything there. I wonder if Natalie knows."

"It might be time to give her a call and tell her you'll be a detained a while longer."

"You're totally right. Shitfuckshit." My hand flew to my mouth. "Sorry. My mouth gets the best of me when I'm stressed."

Mary laughed. "No need to apologize, Kyle's not always the princely councilman he makes himself out to be."

"Mom . . . " there was a bit of playful warning in his voice.

"I was there for the teen years, remember? Charity, I suggest you go ahead and make that call. You'll feel better once you do. And I'm going to send Emma a message. She's always on that phone of hers, so I wonder if she knows about this hashtag you mentioned."

"Of course. I'll call her right now. I can't believe I didn't know this happened first thing, I swear I'm usually on top of things."

Kyle's dimple-smirk returned and I felt myself blush, which was ridiculous; it was a perfectly normal and *non*-dirty phrase, and not unlike when he'd said it. I ignored his reaction, even though my mind was now heading in the same direction as his seemed to be.

"It probably doesn't seem like it now, but I'm very straightforward with a can-do attitude. And I believe honesty is almost always the best policy."

"We don't need any convincing sweetie. You go ahead and make that call."

"Right." Was I stalling? I wasn't one to stall. I charged. And yet, calling Natalie and telling her I wouldn't be there until THE WEDDING DAY? I was not looking forward to this conversation. It wasn't necessarily that I didn't believe in Natalie's capabilities, but I was missing out being at the forefront of a pivotal event. I'd worked hard for this, and I was afraid I wouldn't be seen as capable if I wasn't present most of the weekend. What if it meant they wouldn't come away with a positive view of Satin & Splendor? And what in the actual fuck was I supposed to do with myself stuck in a small town until the road cleared? Still, all those musings aside, my present company was correct: I couldn't put this off. I blew out a breath and took out my phone. Natalie picked up on the fourth ring—she was usually a first ring kind of girl, so that didn't help my nerves.

"Charity! Hi!" She said somewhat breathlessly if not extra-exuberantly. "Are you okay? Is everything alright?"

"Natalie. . . . are *you* okay? You sound like you just ran up three flights of steps."

"Yes, yes of course!" There was some muffled movement then, and it sounded like Natalie covered the phone with her hand. I heard her speak, but couldn't make out what she was saying.

"Nat?"

Then she was back.

"Hi. Yes. Everything is fine. Just staying busy making sure I get those lists checked off."

"Great! Excellent. Happy to hear it. Sooo . . . " I let the word drag out. "I have some news."

"Go on."

"I need you to sit down."

"O . . . kay . . . "

I gave her a second to presumedly do just that, then went ahead and dropped the bomb in one swift spiel. "I'm not sure I'm going to make it. At least not before the wedding. I've been a bit vague on the details before now and I apologize. You were right about the storm: it caught me off guard and I crashed my car."

"Holy shit! JACKIE?!"

I couldn't help but smile at that. I'd spent months deciding on that car. There were lists, of course, but also spreadsheets and even a PowerPoint, all of which I shared with Natalie. She was almost as invested in Jackie as I was, and I appreciated her concern for the vehicle—even if it came before concern for MY wellbeing. Honestly, if the roles were reversed I'd have probably responded the same way.

"I know. But I'm hoping the damage isn't that bad. The thing is, I haven't been able to get it towed, it's still stuck in the snow up on a hill. And as I'm sure you can see, the storm isn't over yet. Also . . . I'm not sure if you've heard, but the wind knocked a giant tree down over the road to the manor. That means not only am I stuck down here but *you're* all stuck up there!"

There was silence for a beat and I had the sudden urge to bite my nails nervously, a habit I'd kicked as a teenager. I wrapped my free hand around the mug Kyle put in front of me to keep it occupied. More gratitude was definitely due once I got done with this conversation; he'd been so helpful. So gracious. So had his mom.

I was sure it was only a second or two that passed in silence, but it felt like an eternity and a half. Was she about to quit? Was Natalie about to tell me this was all too much and she was done and fuck the Hannigans and I could find her relaxing in the hotel hot tub whenever I got there?

"I've got it."

"Excuse me?" I must have misheard.

"I've got this, Charity. You've given me all the information I need, and you already put a lot of things in place. There's nothing for you to do from wherever you are. Speaking of which, *where* are you?"

"This small town called Auburn Falls."

"Oh! I remember passing through on my way up here! It was so cute the way it appeared once you crested the top of a hill that . . . Oh. *That* hill. Damn."

"Yes, that hill."

"Okay. Well, I hope the car is okay. And I'm glad *you're* okay. You *are* okay, aren't you? But of course you are. Did you get a hotel room?"

"Hmm it's not the hotel sort of town. I stayed at someone's home."

"'Someone' like, a stranger??"

I looked up at Kyle who was facing away from me, talking quietly with his mom.

"I mean, we were strangers yesterday, sure, but now? Well, we know each other's names."

"Oh my god. Charity. Okay . . . are you sure you're safe? Say 'banana' if you're in danger."

"I'm fine, Natalie. Apart from my worry over the wedding weekend that is. You know how important it is to the company."

"I do. I know this will be hard for you to hear but you have no control over this Charity, and I really *do* have everything handled. The staff at the manor is also more than proficient."

If only she knew how many times I'd been told I had no control in the last day. I stifled a sigh as more muffled sounds came from the other end of the phone. "What's going on over there?"

"You have to trust me."

"I do trust you!"

Natalie's laugh rang out. "No, you most certainly do not. But now you've got no choice."

"What am I going to do with myself stuck here for god knows how long?!"

"You could try relaxing?"

My silence said more about my thoughts on that front than any words could, and Natalie laughed again.

"Okay, okay. How about having some fun, then? Enjoy the season. It *is* almost Christmas after all."

"You know what's fun for me Nat? Working. Working is fun."

I caught Kyle and Mary give each other a look. It wasn't the first time people thought my work ethic was a bit extreme, but I didn't care.

"Well, I'm all out of ideas, boss. But you'd do well to remember last year's stress-induced panic attack and relax a bit. And one thing I know for sure is this: one way or another, the Hannigan weekend will take place, and you don't have to worry about it. I got this. Now, I've got to go. There's a pile of lists somewhere to try and check off before tonight's welcome dinner. Byee!"

I pursed my lips. I was about to tell her I wasn't a fan of a couple things she'd just said, namely referencing the stress freakout I experienced ONCE, her "one way or another" comment and "try and check off—don't try: do. Precisely as prescribed. That's what I *wanted* to say at least, but she'd already ended the call.

"Okay, well, sounds good. Check in with me later. Bye." I said to absolutely no one. I'd have to talk to her later about hanging up like that.

"Well? How'd it go?" Mary asked. I looked at the phone for a moment in a bit of shock at Natalie's calm, collected manner, then put it down. Kyle leaned on the island with his arms crossed in front of his chest and looked at me expectantly. His gaze made me want to squirm, and I wasn't positive whether it was from nerves or something else entirely.

"Um, pretty well actually. She said she's got it under control." I took a sip of the drink and let out a pleased moan at the delicious flavors and subtle warming from the whiskey as well as the temperature. Kyle's lips twitched at the reaction, just as Mary clapped her hands together happily.

"Wonderful! That's great news, isn't it?! You must be so proud to have built such a strong company and have employees you can lean on. After all your hard work I'm sure you deserve to take a step back and focus on other things. Time for more cardinal sightings," she smiled.

"Having Natalie in control is certainly better than the alternative," I answered, ignoring Kyle. "I wouldn't want a black mark on the company."

I was thrilled Natalie seemed to be handling her first solo event with apparent ease, but I'd never, ever, ever, not been 100 percent involved with my events and available for my clients. It was an odd sensation. I wasn't fond of the lack of control, and now I possessed something I hadn't in a very, very long time. I almost couldn't get the phrase out, it was such a foreign concept, which was exactly how I preferred it. But here I was, and here *it* was, staring me in the face: free time.

Satin & Splendor was in charge of the New Year's Eve Gala at the Boston Ritz, but now in our third year, it practically took care of itself; everything had been organized months ago. I'd worked to keep our schedule light this week so all our energy could focus on the Hannigan wedding, but now I wished I hadn't been quite so efficient. I closed my laptop, put my notebook on top of it, and looked from Mary to Kyle, who was munching unbothered on a handful of nuts.

"Well . . . now what do I do?"

11

"Stay with us through Christmas."

"What?" Kyle and I said together, surprise mirrored on both our faces.

"Mom, as soon as the weather clears and she's able, I'm sure she has family to head back to if she can't make it to the manor."

My stomach roiled at the thought of not making it in time, but what could I do?

"Well, do you?"

"Hmm?"

"Have family to spend Christmas with, assuming you could head off in time to meet them?"

"Let it be known I've not given up *all* hope I'll get to that manor before the wedding, present setbacks aside. But *if* that didn't happen, there's no way I'd impose. I'm sure you two are ready to have me out of your hair, and I plan to leave as soon as I can."

"Optimistic after all" Kyle said, somewhat surprised.

"That doesn't answer the question, dear." Mary fixed me with a stare over the rim of her glasses. Coupled with the silver hair coiled on top of her head and the festive sweater she wore covered in embroidered presents, I couldn't help but compare her to a stern Mrs. Claus.

"Well . . . no. Not this year." Not any year, in fact. Not since the Christmas after we lost dad.

"Then there we have it! You should stay."

I looked at Kyle and wondered whether he'd push for me to leave— I didn't want to stick around if he was counting the minutes until I'd be gone. "What do you think?"

He pulled plates from the cupboard, and Mary added generous pieces of lasagna, a slice of warm bread, and a serving of salad.

"As it stands, I think you don't have much of a choice in the matter," he said with a shrug.

"That's true . . . so maybe we should just take it as it comes?"

"Seems fair enough. Right mom?"

"Oh, fine. I suppose so." She appeared dejected for a moment, then reset as she brought the steaming plates of food to the island. "Well, anyway, for now—we eat."

We gathered around and enjoyed a delicious meal that hit the spot exactly like Mary said it would. She never got around to making dessert to go with it, but she promised we'd be doing some baking together since I was staying longer, something I wasn't sure whether to look forward to or dread. It'd been years since I baked anything. Heck, it'd been years since I'd done a lot of things except work, but that wasn't a complaint. It was, once again, precisely how I wanted things.

By the time we finished eating, the snow had let up a bit more, and Kyle decided he'd be up for another trip to town after all. He mentioned needing a few things he refused to specify about, but I had a feeling in the end, he really just wanted to bring his sister some food.

"I'd ask if you want to join," he'd said, "but after this morning's escapade I figured you might want to stay inside where it's warm and dry," he finished with a smirk. "Are those boots the only pair you brought?"

"Yeah, I wasn't expecting to be outside much. My other shoes are also impractical: flats and some heels. Oh! Also a pair of sneakers for the gym I thought I'd be using, but now that I think of it I forgot those in the car."

"I had a feeling," he nodded and headed off, leaving me curled up on one of the big chairs beside the fire. Mary refused to let me help clean, and directed me instead to the bookshelf. I chose a novel that seemed somewhat interesting, but didn't make it past the first page before I put it down and picked up my phone instead. I couldn't avoid it any longer.

I went on the S&S Instagram to find Natalie had posted some updates to stories. There were also several notifications, but I clicked on the story icon to give myself a warm-up before I braved whatever others might be saying or sharing.

As first one image, then another, and another, followed by a couple short videos flashed in front of my eyes, my heart sped up . . . with thrill! The images were divine. A hand flew to my mouth and relief flooded through me. Everything looked perfect! Natalie was doing exactly as I taught her: showing just enough to tease all we were capable of, but not enough to give everything away. We prided ourselves on curating events people had to attend to fully experience. We encouraged selective sharing—we knew any posts were essentially free publicity, but we also told the guests at our events, "If they were meant to be here, they would have received an invite."

So far, Natalie decided to stick with detail shots. Some images showed items from the day's various activities: a cigar next to a glass of whiskey, resting on top of one of the monogrammed cocktail napkins; a palate of paint and a brush next to the corner of a completed canvas; a cocktail glass and some perfectly placed ingredients. I let out a laugh as the next image appeared, showing the personalized towels and toiletries in the bathrooms.

To most, the sight of them would have little to no meaning. Toiletries—big deal. But it was yet another reminder Natalie had been paying attention, and a forever memory of one of the lessons I'd learned as a fledgling planner.

The Hannigan wedding included a small but select set, yet despite the literal size, it would still be a huge affair thanks to social media, the family's connections, and the inevitable publicity to follow. Everything needed to be perfect, down to the most minute detail. After all, anyone with a phone—so *everyone*—was a potential PR associate. I considered this mostly a positive, but you could never say for sure what would catch someone's attention, so you had to cover all your bases twice over, and then lift them up and take care of underneath, too.

I thought back to the wedding from my amateur days; one of the guests had a following online from her posts about freaken bathrooms, of all things. I'd made the mistake of assuming those weren't my purview—surely whatever venue we were at would handle *that* business.

It was a terrible mistake.

She posted a photo of one of the stalls with an empty toilet paper rack and the caption, "I wonder if the bride will lend me some tulle?"

I was mortified, and learned my lesson: don't depend on others. There was a reason my sole tattoo was a tiny crab from *The Little Mermaid* on my ankle. It was my constant reminder of the phrase he'd said: *If you want something done, you've got to do it yourself.*

After that, depending on the scale of the event, I always included bathrooms in my decor considerations. Bouquets, baskets of toiletries, monogrammed towels the couple could help design and keep—after I sent them the dry cleaners, of course—and beyond.

And now, I had my own saying: *did you do two in the bathrooms?* In other words, were they checked twice?

Clearly, Natalie did just that.

Feeling enthused now, I clicked through to some of the posts we'd been tagged in. I held my breath as I checked the first few, but let it go when I realized they were all positive; more images shared about the day's activities and decor details with raving captions underneath. Sarabeth insisted on a winter wonderland theme, even though her mother wanted something more traditional, and I was glad her daughter won out. It looked truly magical, and everyone appeared to be having an amazing time. I knew appearances could be deceiving, especially on social media, but I crossed my fingers it was going as well in real life.

A new image popped up while I was scrolling from the S&S account. I clicked over and found a picture of a fallen-down tree already covered in a layer of snow. The image looked festive and artsy, and the caption put a grin on my face. It read:

The Hannigans asked for a secluded, intimate affair—one that wouldn't be interrupted by would-be event crashers or paparazzi—and when S&S makes a promise, we deliver! Good luck getting by our "gate"!

That girl. Natalie was definitely up for a raise and promotion after all this. I sent her a quick text.

Me: Brilliant spin on the tree! Beat 'em to the punch!

I'd been afraid once word got out there was a tree blocking the road the media would paint a picture of a frightened wedding party trapped in a remote manor which was *not* what we wanted. But Natalie's post, in which she tagged Sarabeth and some other attendees with a significant following, was already being shared. The media wouldn't be able to squeeze drama out of it now!

I put my phone aside with a relieved sigh and eyed the nearby sofa. I never napped—why waste perfectly good daylight?—but what was the harm in laying down for a minute or two? My belly was full, the fire warmed the room and crackled comfortingly, Mary had instrumental Christmas music playing in another room, and everything I'd just seen resulted in a huge weight lifted off my shoulders. Not all of it, of course, but enough for me to feel like I could relax, if only for a bit. Everything was cozy and peaceful. Just a minute or two, I told myself, and I rose from the chair, stretched on the sofa, fluffed a pillow with a painted Christmas tree on it and placed it under my head.

"That's what this room is missing," I said to myself, stifling a yawn. "A Christmas tree."

I turned on my side and watched the flames dance in the fireplace—it was the last thing I saw before my eyelids grew heavy.

12

I woke with a start to find myself covered with a warm blanket and was instantly appalled at myself. I'd taken a nap! This place was completely shifting my usual patterns. I took stock of the situation: the fire was still going, and I could still hear music, so maybe it hadn't been all that long. I stood and stretched, folded the blanket Mary must have put on me, that sweet woman, and returned to the chair. I wasn't sure why I was embarrassed at the thought of Kyle catching me snoozing, but I hoped the nap had been short and he was still in town. That hope fizzled out a moment later when I glanced at my phone's lock screen to learn I'd been asleep for more than two hours! I picked up the book I'd selected and tried reading it again.

"You get very far?" I jumped at the sound of Kyle's voice, looked up and tried to fix him with a wide-awake kind of gaze, whatever that meant. I probably looked like a deer in headlights. Gosh, why did he have to be so good-looking, and why did I have to notice so much?

"Whoa, sorry about that. I didn't mean to startle you."

"It's okay." My voice was raspy from sleep. I cleared my throat to try and get rid of my nap's evidence. Maybe he'd just gotten back? "And um, not really. I couldn't stand it any longer and had to check social media."

"And?"

"Annnd I'm happy to say everything looks like it's going great! Of course, I really have no idea if it *actually* is. Social media versus real life and all that, but it should do the trick PR-wise. What do you have there?"

He walked over and handed me a bag. "For you."

"What?" Well *that* was unexpected. I reached in and pulled out a pair of winter boots.

"For function, not fashion," Kyle said with a shrug.

"Actually, they're kind of cute!" I said as I looked them over, in a bit of disbelief at the thoughtfulness. "But you didn't have to do this! And wait, how did you know my size??"

He stood beside the fireplace and held his hands over the flame. "I checked those things you call boots that you left by the door before heading out. And I know I didn't, but I couldn't have you falling in any more icy streams."

"Wow. Thank you so much. That was really thoughtful."

In a moment of impulse I stood and stepped over to give him a hug. As my arms went to wrap around his waist, I wondered if I was still half asleep: what the eff I was doing? But it was too late to back out. Kyle hesitated just a fraction of a second—still enough for me to notice, which made embarrassment lump in with everything else at my spontaneity—then he wrapped his arms around me in return and pulled me against him.

His warmth surrounded me immediately, along with that fresh air scent. It was not an undesirable combination and cemented this was in fact a dangerous choice. I let go and took a step back. Okay. Regroup. It was just a friendly hug. Not like I ran up and kissed him over a pair of boots . . . but now I was *thinking* about kissing him, and heat rose to my cheeks. What was wrong with me? And since when was I a hugger?!

I let out a nervous laugh and tucked some hair behind my ear.

"Sorry, was that excessive? You'd think I'd never been given a pair of shoes before. Although, come to think of it, I don't think I have been!"

There was that signature grin. "Well, if it makes you this happy, you should get them more often. You'll have to tell me how to reach your boyfriend so I can drop him a hint."

"Oh, I . . . " Was this his way of finding out if I was single? It was pretty smooth, honestly. I was about to tell him Darren wasn't really a big gifter, or maybe it was just that I was hard to buy for since I usually bought whatever I wanted . . . and then I remembered. "Actually I'm not seeing anyone."

The first time I'd said those words in seven years. And perhaps it was odd, but I didn't say them with any sense of sadness.

"Ah," Kyle answered, then appeared contemplative for a moment. He took a seat in the chair opposite mine, so I sat down again too. "So!

I was thinking . . . "

I eyed him curiously. "Careful, that can be dangerous."

He waved a hand dismissively. "How often do you relax?"

I laughed. "Never if I can help it. It may not seem like it at present but I like staying busy. Don't let my earlier breakfast nook reverie fool you: sitting around isn't usually my cup of cocoa."

"Cup of cocoa! I'm starting to think a stopover in this town is exactly what you need. You're getting in the spirit already!"

"Yeah well it's not like I have anything else to do," I bemoaned.

"Exactly. That's it!"

I eyed him warily. "What's it?"

"Well, we may have only known each other a short while, but I can already tell you've got more lists than Santa."

"So?" I bristled, waiting for a snide remark about women in the workforce.

"No, no need to get defensive," he said, reading me immediately. Another disarming feature. "I didn't say it was a bad thing, just an observation."

"Okay . . . "

"Well, I don't want you to go stir crazy, sitting around with a nervous bouncing knee, tapping your pencil irritably on the table . . . "

"I don't do either of those things!"

"But you might pick up both habits if we're not careful."

I harrumphed. "Not likely."

"Even so, how about I set you up with a different sort of list to follow? I can't stand to see you sitting here, practically feverish you can't check off more on your lists."

"Wow, is it really that obvious?"

"It's that obvious."

I'd have to contemplate my expressions later. All this time I thought I had such a tight hold on them. I pressed my lips together. "Well, what did you have in mind?"

"A Christmas list."

"Uh . . . I haven't made a list for Santa in a long time."

"I mean a Christmas BUCKET list. A list of festive things to do. That counts as a list, doesn't it??"

"Well sure, but I told you I don't really celebrate."

"Even more of a reason. We might as well make this unexpected detour enjoyable for you. And your lack of holiday cheer is depressing, honestly. Who doesn't make time for the holidays?!"

"Well I don't live near family, and I usually have events keeping me busy so . . . " For now, I'd leave out the fact it just never felt the same without dad.

He gave me a pointed look. "Decidedly *not* cheerful. Let's give you some things to do to get in the spirit for once and keep you from going downright crazy over unfinished lists and social media posts. Personally I think a bit of downtime would do you some good, too, based on all I know about you. Which I know, I know, isn't much . . . "

I looked at my watch. "Well considering we've still known each other less than a day, I'd say you know an impressive amount, actually . . . " In fact, it was a little unnerving just how much he'd been able to glean about me. At least, he'd already accurately pegged me as a list-obsessed workaholic likely to stress over social posts as well. "It's *you* that's the relative stranger, councilman."

His fingers went through his hair, slightly mussing the way he'd styled it, and I tried not to gawk at the move, which definitely should not look as good as it did nor cause the internal reaction that it did. Couldn't a man move some hair out of his face in peace?? I suddenly wondered at the way Darren and I scheduled *everything*, including sex. Well, perhaps I should say the way *I* scheduled everything. Maybe it hadn't been enough. Considering Darren's current title as EX-boyfriend, and his comments about being "lit up" by the new girl, I had a feeling he'd likely say 'absolutely not.' My mind was usually occupied with too many other things to think over frequency. And as for anything spontaneous? Headspace zero. But now? Now that there was a little more room up there, I had to admit it was starting to meander a bit around *Councilman* Kyle . . .

"There's a town full of people who could tell you anything you want to know." His words brought my focus back to the conversation at hand. "That title means even more of my business gets around than it did before and trust me, it was quite a lot then, too."

"I'd rather hear it from you though," I said with a smile, and the truth to that statement caught me off guard. I *did* want to know this man more, and not only because of his unintentionally attractive hair-moving habits. "If I agree to this Christmasy list idea of yours, you'll have to add some sort of speed dating. That is . . . not that we're looking to date." I felt heat rush to my cheeks again. Why did he make me feel like a decidedly uncool teenager with a crush? "I just mean some sort of 'get to know you' event. We could include your mom too. I feel like I should know a bit more about the people I'm living with for the next however long. What if you're secretly murderers?"

"It's a little late to be worrying about that, don't you think? You already got in my truck, pretty willingly I might add, and let me bring you to a secluded house where you then got out—again willingly—and walked inside of your own accord. If Mother Mary and I were looking to murder you there were quite a few opportunities already."

"That's fair. It sounds like the plot of a holiday horror film, actually. But I decided you were a safe bet because of all the people who came in to The Hearth and knew you. You didn't come across as a shady creep."

He tilted his head. "Well, 'not a shady creep' certainly isn't the most complimentary thing I've been told by a woman, but I suppose I'll take it. Is the bar really that low?"

I laughed at his good humor and decided to give him a bit more. "So I've heard. And, well, you were also relatively charming. I liked how friendly you were. It helps that you're easy on the eyes, too."

"Ah ha! Now we're getting somewhere."

"So what do I get if I finish?"

"Excuse me?"

"I'm a reward kinda gal. I always give myself an incentive for reaching my goals. Jackie was a reward." I pursed my lips. "Although I don't *always* need one; the satisfaction of completion can be reward enough."

Kyle broke into a roar of laughter that confused me for just a moment, until realization dawned and I rolled my eyes at his reaction to more unintentional innuendos.

"Did she agree?" Our entertaining exchange was interrupted by Mary coming down the stairs.

"I think so?" Kyle looked at me questioningly, a laugh still lingering on his lips.

"Mary, you're in on this too?"

She laughed as she approached and placed a hand on the back of Kyle's chair. "Of course I am. Who do you think Kyle got his festive spirit from? And who do you think is going to help ensure the two of you don't burn my house down with the first item on the list?"

"What's the first item on the list?" I asked Kyle, and in answer he produced a folded piece of paper from his pocket. He handed it to me and I leaned back in the chair and opened it.

"Oh, my, goodness. Did you do this yourself? When did you have time to make this??"

It wasn't just words on paper; interspersed throughout the page of various holiday activities were an array of the sweetest little festive watercolor paintings.

"While you were sleeping . . . "

"Oh." So much for only Mary finding me in my unconscious state.

"I thought about dumping snow on you, but mom wouldn't let me," he added with a smirk.

"I guess he didn't inherit hospitality along with the festive spirit?"

Mary shook her head.

"I apologize for falling asleep like that," I added. "I don't typically nap."

My companions looked at me like I was a bit crazy, their resemblance on display through matching expressions.

"You don't nap?"

"Of course not. That's time I could use being productive."

"Naps are productive," Kyle said with absolute certainty.

"Oh are they? How so?"

"Improving brain function. Allowing your body the chance for a midday recharge. You must get grumpy a lot."

"What! I do not!"

"'Think what a better world it would be if we all—the whole world —had cookies and milk about three o'clock every afternoon and then lay down with our blankies for a nap.' Robert Folghum."

"In case you haven't realized, mom's a fan of a good quote."

"As long as there's substance to it. You won't find any 'live, laugh, love' on the walls here."

"I wouldn't expect there to be," I said sincerely. "Not when inside's already filled with more than enough."

Kyle put a hand to his heart. "Wow. Oh wow. Charity, that was positively saccharine."

"You're very sweet, dear," Mary added, and I hoped I wasn't blushing. While the comment was true, it'd flown out of my mouth before I had a chance to stop it, and was, admittedly, not to character. Then again, neither was my cocoa comment. Or the flirting. I focused my attention on the list again.

"These are really lovely. Which one of you added them?"

"I did . . . "

"Before his foray into property and politics, Kyle was quite the artist!" Mary said fondly. "Always creating on any surface he could get. Although when he was a boy, he'd draw on any surface, period.

These walls have had their fair share of art on them."

My surprise must have been written on my face, because Kyle shook his head and laughed. "Don't look so shocked. They're just a couple of Christmas doodles. And I wouldn't call being a councilman in Auburn Falls a 'foray into politics' mom. You also know that's not why I haven't been painting much anymore."

Mary pursed her lips. "Yes, well, you know what I think about anything that no-good little—"

"Yes mom," Kyle cut her off sternly. "I *do* know. Which is why you don't need to repeat it."

There was tension in the air—so unlike the usual ambiance of the place—and I wanted it to clear. Tension only ever reminded me of the feeling in my own home post-diagnosis. I looked at the first item. Color: green. Food.

"Oh no . . ."

Two pairs of eyes turned to me. "What is it?" they asked in unison.

"I do *not* bake."

13

It was not as easy a task as I'm sure they thought it would be. People who know how to bake always think it's the easiest thing, something anyone can just waltz into a kitchen and do.

"Follow the recipe!" they say, then leave out a lot of pertinent information about settling flour and dry versus liquid ingredients and butter temperature and mixing methodology. Maybe it was intentional. Perhaps all bakers had an intrinsic competitive side they hid behind a stack of cupcakes and a smile; act like you're encouraging while keeping anyone else from joining the ranks of baker and putting your own precious title at risk.

At least that was what I'd come to believe about most of them, but Mary was proving me wrong. Despite my professed ineptitude, she did not give up or offer a skip card for this particular item. Instead she relayed some of that aforementioned info. As I went to dip the measuring cup in the jar of flour, she stopped me with a gentle hand on the arm.

"Fluff it with a fork first, spoon it into your cup gently, then level it off." Even better, she added, would be to "weigh it like they do in Europe."

She explained "creamed" butter and sugar did not in fact magically turn to cream, that I should crack eggs on a hard surface instead of the edge of a bowl so I don't push any shells inside, and if, by chance a piece or two fell in the bowl—and yes, a couple did—use a larger piece of shell to scoop them out.

But the clincher was when Mary told me "once you've got the tips and tricks down, baking is simply checking off steps, with a nice reward at the end. That seems right up your alley."

"When you put it like that, it certainly does. It's the 'tips and tricks' part that always hung me up though. I never had anyone teach me those."

"Hmmm," Mary mused. "Not a family of bakers then, I take it?"

"Oh there was baking, it was just more of the slice-and-bake and pop-a-can variety. No need to learn about appropriate flour measurements and all that."

"No shame in the convenience game! It still leads to gathering together in the kitchen, and that's half the fun. Speaking of family, is there a reason they won't be expecting you for the holidays? Snowstorm aside, were you going to be busy at this wedding of yours through Christmas?"

I hesitated only a moment before deciding to answer candidly. Mary was so warm and open, I felt like I could tell her anything. And as for Kyle, well, I got the same vibe from him, I just found myself feeling reserved as a result of *feeling* in general. I focused solely on Mary as I replied and ignored the fact Kyle was sitting nearby.

"We actually haven't spent the holidays together in a long time. It's just my brother and my mom and me and we do our own thing." I paused then, because it wasn't really just the three of us at all anymore. "Actually, that's not entirely true. My mom is married, and the two of them go on a cruise for Christmas every year. My brother has a family of his own now, so he does the holidays with them. They live in California. Annnd all the festive fanfare seems silly for two." I screwed up my lips as I wondered how long it'd take to remember it was just me now. "Well . . . for one, this year. Just further incentive to work straight through."

It wasn't the entire story, but no lie either. I added the wet ingredients Mary set in front of me and blended them together as I spoke. "But that makes it easier to take on events this time of year. There's no one I need to make excuses for. There was my ex, but I'd been under the impression we both preferred working through the holidays. I only learned that wasn't the case when we broke up yesterday." I simultaneously laughed and shrugged as I said the last part, then felt embarrassment rise at what was most likely an overshare. "That was probably a more in-depth answer than you were looking for. Sorry about that."

"Don't apologize; the answer I was looking for was whatever you felt like sharing." She placed a hand on my shoulder. "Thank you for opening up like that."

It was an odd sensation being thanked for sharing and having someone say they were interested in the details of my life. I was used to professional pleasantries and brief answers to "how are you?" and "what's going on?" All generic replies that didn't really get into the nitty gritty. When's the last time I gave genuine answers that moved beyond the surface? I knew most people didn't care for an in-depth response. My clients didn't really want to know, and that was how it should be. Despite how friendly we might get during our time together, I was an employee. Natalie was the closest thing I had to a real friend, but I doubted she viewed me as such—I was her boss, after all—but she knew more about my life than most.

"Alright, back to cookies?" I asked to shift the conversation.

And so, under Mary's watchful eye I found myself baking actual freaken Christmas cookies. Well, more accurately, *their* watchful eye. Kyle hung back while Mary showed me the ropes, sitting at the island, pretending to browse a newspaper like some sort of grandpa. And I knew he was pretending, because on more than one occasion I caught him watching us. During one such catch, our eyes met and he had the nerve to wink, and then I had the nerve to feel flustered, and poured a little too much into the bowl, resulting in a cloud of dry ingredients as the mixer whirred around.

"Whoops!" Mary said good-heartedly, lowering the speed until the flour fog cleared. Kyle chuckled, then brought the paper up to cover his grin.

"Are you just going to sit there or are you going to help?" Mary asked her son.

"Not if you like your kitchen."

She put her hands on her hips.

"If I get involved we'll probably have to call the fire department, and I can't say how long it'll be until they get here in this weather."

Mary harrumphed and turned her focus back to me, but my own mind began to wander; I couldn't help but admire their relationship, and felt a pang at the lack of contact I'd had with my own family. I wasn't even sure what my brother was doing this year, or where mom was adventuring to. Dad's death broke us, and we scattered like shattered glass; pieces far too small and numerous to reform, I always told myself. But what if I'd been wrong?

"Alright. Next, the dough chills." Mary said as she shut off the mixer, and my thoughts along with it.

"And so do we?" I asked hopefully.

"Not quite, that's just the sugar cookie dough! Next up: cranberry chocolate chip, and now that I've shown you the basics, you two are doing this batch yourselves!"

"But Kyle said—"

"Don't you mind what Kyle said, he's been helping me in the kitchen his whole life alongside his sister. The problem is he gets bored and distracted during the actual baking part, but I have a feeling you'll do just fine keeping track of the time. No burnt cookies on your watch! Now, I'm off to finish my crossword."

And with that, she snatched the paper from Kyle's hands and headed for the living room. Kyle jumped up in the aftermath and clapped his hands together enthusiastically, startling me in the process.

"Alright! Let's do this!"

"Jesus!" I said, my hand flying to my heart.

"Yep! He's the reason for the season!" Kyle opened a drawer and pulled out an apron of his own. The front read "whatever happens, we're eating it."

"Oh that's comforting," I laughed. "There's not another one to match mine?"

I twirled, showing off my own red apron edged in white à la Santa's suit.

"Nope, and I don't think I could pull if off quite as well as you."

"Thanks. So what's first?"

"Beats me. These are your cookies, I'm just here to supervise. The recipe is next to the bowl of cranberries."

"I'm not doing this by myself—this is your list, after all!"

"Actually, it's *your* list, I'm just the one who wrote it."

"And decorated it."

He nodded in concession. "And decorated it."

"Ok. First up: cream the butter and sugar."

"See? You're already getting the hang of this."

I gave him a smile. "I guess I am, aren't I?"

"You'll put Mrs. Claus out of business in no time."

❄❄❄

We did not, in fact, burn down Mary's kitchen. Without her

supervision, things got a bit messier than they probably would have with her nearby, but the most important thing is the fire department was never required. And the cookies? They turned out absolutely delicious, which ended up being the ultimate surprise, although Kyle and Mary seemed to have more confidence in me than I did myself. It was an odd sensation: feeling nervous about an outcome and outside my element. I'd spent years curating an environment where I felt in control, where I was practically guaranteed to excel, and I'd thrived in that milieu.

But a nagging voice started up because of a few trays of darn Christmas cookies: was I missing out by not letting myself loosen the reins now and then? By being afraid to try new things? I thought of Darren's words. Of sushi. Of Natalie's comments. Heck, even Kyle and his assertion I needed to embrace more of the festive spirit. Were they right? I tried to shove that voice aside. My way of doing things had served me well for more than a decade, so why change now?

The "bake Christmas cookies" check hadn't been earned yet, despite making a double batch of two different types. Mary surprised Kyle and me by adding another element to the task, so after the last sugar cookie was decorated and cooled, I found myself back in Kyle's truck holding onto several cookie tins. As we drove along, I realized a slight smile was stuck on my face, and I knew it was from more than the cookies.

Baking with Kyle was hilarious. He'd turned on Christmas music while we worked, and sang along to more songs than not. He'd made us more cocoa. And, despite his assertion he wouldn't be much help, when it came time to cut out the chilled dough and I couldn't quite get the hang of my first time rolling it out—it kept getting stuck to the pin and I couldn't get it thin enough—he stepped in to help.

Or, more accurately, he stepped *behind me* to help. My awkward hug aside, it was the closest we'd been since he'd helped me out of the frozen stream. His arms appeared beside me, sweater sleeves pushed up to his elbows like his shirt had been that first night. Had I ever found forearms so attractive before? The smell of the chocolate cranberry cookies already in the oven mingled with his fresh air scent. It became hard to swallow.

"Is this okay?" He'd asked, and I nodded.

He rubbed flour over the rolling pin to help with the sticking, then placed his hands on top of mine at either end and showed me the best way to roll it out.

"Start at the middle," he said. "Then press gently, work your way out, rotate and repeat."

He was talking about cookie dough. COOKIE DOUGH. There was absolutely nothing sexual about the words coming out of his mouth and yet my mind found a way to twist things around, making it so I started thinking of things that were decidedly *not* related to holiday baking.

Was I delusional? Going crazy? My relationship with Darren had been . . . well, I wouldn't say sexually barren, but we were so busy! Or had that not really been it at all? I thought again of our last conversation. Had I been oblivious to the true state of our relationship? Had I been too busy to truly see? And when had the things Darren said ever made me react like *this*? I certainly never found a way to turn his comments about numbers into something sex-related. It had to be the fact I wasn't as busy as I usually was, and I wasn't quite sure whether it was good or bad. Yet to be determined? All I knew for sure was that Kyle's hands on top of mine and his scent surrounding me warmed me more than the 375 degree oven. And his instruction ended way too soon.

He cleared his throat, grabbed the cookie cutters then moved to stand beside me. There was something in the air between us, and it wasn't just the aroma of fresh-baked cookies.

When our festive shapes had been cut and the first tray placed in the oven in exchange for the last of the chocolate cranberry, Mary came back and fixed us both with a smile.

"I could smell the cookies from the living room. They look perfect! Mrs. Rogers, Mr. Fuller, and the Gallagher family will love them. Once they're cooled can you—"

"Wait," Kyle interrupted, "We're giving them away?!"

"Well not all of them dear, but of course! I always bake cookies for the neighbors, but you're usually out and about when I deliver them. There's a couple batches already on the hutch in the dining room I've been hiding from you."

Kyle gave Mary a faux affronted look. *"You've been hiding cookies from me?!"*

Mary patted her son lovingly on the cheek. "You'll be alright. Once we pack up the tins I'll leave out all that's left for your insatiable sweet tooth. I thought you and Charity could deliver them this year?"

He'd given me a look, and I'd shrugged.

"What else have I got to do? I mean, apart from my list that is. Speaking of which, have you settled on a reward yet?"

"You haven't realized yet that the list *is* the gift? Tsk. You're going to be a harder nut to crack than I thought."

"I disagree," Mary added. "I think she'll fully embrace the spirit before we know it." She held up a tray of cookies. "I mean, look at this! Holiday perfection! Now. Let's start prepping our icing. Kyle, grab the sprinkles, would you?!"

My eyes had gone wide. "Wait, there's more?!"

14

"What are you smiling about?"

Kyle's question brought me back to the truck.

"Oh, I was just thinking about what fun I had baking today."

Naturally, I left out just how much of those thoughts centered around him . . . was that nuts? I'd known him less than a day and yet admittedly felt more comfortable with him and his mom—more open —than I had with anyone in quite a long time. In fact, it was an openness and vulnerability I wasn't sure I'd experienced since my dad was still alive. He'd always been the one I talked to. I told him everything.

"You're my best buddy," I was known for telling him from a young age, and it was a badge he wore proudly.

The roads were still snow-laden, and flakes continued to dance around as we made our way to the neighbors.

"Mom uses the term "neighbor" loosely," Kyle explained. "They surround our house, sure, but they're each a few miles away. Even so, if it wasn't weathering so much, we could walk through the woods to their homes. That's what I used to do when I'd visit Mike—the Gallaghers are his parents."

"It must be peaceful out here with all this land separating the homes. I've been in Boston since college, and I absolutely love it there, but this is nice too."

"What about growing up? Did you live in a city?"

"No, the suburbs—a town more developed than here though. My first house was a pretty quintessential American home, in fact: white picket fence and all. It was yellow with white shutters, lovely gardens, and a pretty tree out front on a cul-de-sac. But we moved when I was a teenager."

"Do you miss it?"

I looked out the window and thought for a moment. Memories flashed like someone was scrolling through a movie, and with them came a bittersweet pang.

"I do. Not because of the actual house or the picket fence or any of that stuff. But the memories."

"I can understand that," Kyle nodded, and for once I felt like the understanding was true due to our shared loss of a parent. I wondered if he'd ever feel like opening up about his dad.

We pulled up to our first house, and marched through the snow to deliver a pretty tin of cookies to a very grateful household who sent us off with a Christmas loaf in return. The second neighbor was Mrs. Rogers, who was quite surprised we were out and about considering the weather. She invited us in for a drink, which I expected to be coffee or tea, but was amused to discover was a round of gin martinis. Afterwards, we were given several mason jars of Chex mix and went on our way with Kyle promising to be along once the snow was over to clear her walkway.

We headed to our final stop then, where Mr. Fuller acted like we'd been traveling in the winter weather all day, and insisted we come in to "sit a spell" and warm up. When we left an hour later, after being given cheese and crackers and a mug of mulled wine I raved about, it was with my own jar of mulling spices.

As we sat in the truck afterwards, I found myself in awe of the friendliness and hospitality of the people we'd met. That's not to say I didn't come in contact with friendly people in the city—I loved Bostonians—but there was something so wholesome and old-timey about the interactions we'd just had.

"Gone again, I see . . . or am I such terrible company?"

I turned to Kyle. "Oh, not at all! This time I was just thinking about how nice everybody is. The whole town is like this?"

"Oh don't let them—or maybe I should say *us*—fool you. This is a town of trouble makers, thieves, and liars."

I rolled my eyes. "I doubt that."

"They're gossips at least. One of this town's favorite hobbies. Some rumors are probably being spread as we speak about who you are and what we're doing driving around town together with tins of cookies in a snowstorm."

My eyes widened at the thought and Kyle laughed, clearly amused at my expense. "But maybe the thieves and liars part is a bit untrue, although I admit I stole a candy from Clark's Groceries once."

"You didn't!"

He gave me a remorseful look. "I did. My dad told me I couldn't have one. I rebelled."

The mention of his dad caught me off guard. It was the first time he'd said anything about him. "Did you get caught?"

"Guilt had me confessing later. He brought me back and had me tell the manager, who just so happened to be father of the girl I'd had a crush on. So I ruined my chances with her because of a darned candy bar. There was no way he was about to let his daughter date a criminal."

"Oh my god, that's got to be an exaggeration."

"Nope. But it all turned out for the best. She was meant to be with Will Jones. They've got the sweetest little postcard family now. . . . So I take it you haven't noticed yet?"

"Noticed what?"

He nodded toward the windshield and I looked outside. It was dark out. We'd baked away the afternoon, and the winter sun liked her early bedtime. His headlights illuminated the snowy road in front of us. I was about to tell him I didn't know what he was referring too and I didn't see anything out of the ordinary, when I realized what I *wasn't* seeing was precisely the point: there were no more snowflakes dancing in the lights.

"It stopped snowing!"

"It appears that way. And earlier than expected, too! That means the boys will be hard at work getting these roads clear for morning."

Did that mean I'd be able to leave? Would I be able to make it in time for the wedding?

"Oh wow. I need to reach out to Natalie. I wonder how long it'll take to dig out my car. I'm sure nothing broke mechanically. I was as careful as I could be when I turned it off the road; any physical damage I could always take care of later."

I pulled out my notebook and started looking at the schedule. I glanced at the clock, noted the rehearsal dinner was already underway, and couldn't help the pang of disappointment that cropped up again at missing all the events.

"Easy there, Cherry. You're getting a little ahead of yourself. I think you're forgetting something."

"What am I—wait, did you just call me Cherry?"

"Uh, yes. Yes I did. It sort of just came out," he laughed sheepishly. "Sorry?"

I found myself laughing at his expression of remorse, even as a different kind of pang shot through me. In all my years, no one had thought to change Charity to Cherry. That is, apart from my dad, who fondly called me his Cherry Berry. My dad . . . and now Kyle.

"It's fine. Anyway, what am I forgetting?"

"One very large tree."

"Oh." I felt the energy that started to buzz through me settle, and I deflated a little against the seat. "You're right. The tree."

"But I'm sure they'll get to work on it as soon as they can tomorrow," he added hurriedly. "Then you can scamper away from here without so much as a backward glance."

"I'm not sure I've ever 'scampered' before Kyle."

Did I sense disappointment in his voice? There were things I wanted to ask him. Things that were throwing me off guard. Like how amid the excitement at potentially making my way to the Hannigan wedding after all, *I'd* felt a dash of disappointment at the thought of leaving. And when he reminded me of the tree, the feelings flipped: excitement at staying longer, disappointment at missing Satin & Splendor's event of the year.

Did Kyle feel any of those conflicting feels? And was it wild and crazy to have them when you'd known a person for less than a day? I looked again at the clock on the dash: this time yesterday I was making my way to the restaurant, which made it *almost a day*.

Although, how was chatting with a stranger in person and then deciding there was a bit of attraction and you wanted to get to know them better any different from chatting with someone on a dating app and deciding the same?

"Well, we'll just have to wait and see what tomorrow brings," Kyle declared. "Are you hungry?"

I had a number of follow-up questions, but his sudden change of topic had me pushing them aside.

"A little . . . what'd you have in mind?"

"We could head back to town, I want to check on the status of the blackout, and there might be a chance The Hearth is open either way. If it is, I'm sure Toni would take care of us."

"Let's do it. That shepherd's pie *was* pretty delicious. But will your mom be making dinner? Should we bring something back for her?"

"You're thinking of my mom?" Kyle gave me that endearing smile of his. "That's really sweet Cherry."

"Well, if you've learned anything about me during our short acquaintance, it should be that I like to —"

"Be in control because you're afraid of what could happen if you're not?"

"I . . . no. Wait, what? I was going to say I like to have all my bases covered."

Kyle nodded his head like that was a valid answer as well. "That too. And this really has been a short acquaintance, hasn't it? It feels longer, somehow."

I remained silent, even though I was tempted to agree. But I was still mulling over what he'd said just before that. *Afraid of what could happen.* A part of me wanted to be annoyed at him for saying it, but was it wrong? I knew the answer. I just didn't want to admit it.

We pulled into the parking lot to find the establishment lit from within.

"Looks like that answers the question about it being open or not. Let's see who couldn't be kept away because of a little snow. Rachel's cooking is pretty irresistible. This is also basically the only place to hang out in town after dark. . . . how are those boots holding up by the way?" he asked as we headed for the door.

"Really well, thanks. And if I didn't say it before—nice choice!" I kicked back my leg to raise the faux-fur lined boot.

"It's called 'balancing fashion with function,'" he grinned and held open the door. "Or so my sister said—she helped me pick them out. You were missing the function part before."

"Yeah. Well, I wasn't expecting all this snowy traipsing."

Kyle took my coat as I shrugged out of it and hung it on one of the pegs beside the entry. The ambiance was much the same as the night before: warm, cozy, and lively. The voice of Bing Crosby could be heard over the chatter. Dinner scents mixed with cinnamon and citrus and acted as a greeting that set my stomach rumbling.

"Bar or table?" Kyle asked, but I was saved from answering—a good thing since my mind had quickly begun whirring through the pros and cons of each—when we entered the main room to find most of the tables once again occupied.

"I guess the snow didn't keep anyone away today either," I said. "So much for that 'stay home' suggestion your mom mentioned.'"

"Yeah, 'suggestion' is the key word there," Kyle laughed.

"Intimate dates must not be a thing in this town," I added.

"Not really . . . is that what you were hoping for, Ms. Evans?"

I turned to find an eyebrow raised mischievously.

"I . . . no. I mean, we just . . . I was speaking generally."

How did this man have the ability to turn me into a blubbering fool? It was *not* my typical M.O. Thank goodness Natalie had gone on ahead and wasn't stuck here with me; if she saw how I was acting she'd think the real Charity was abducted by aliens and I was an imposter. Or maybe I hit my head harder than I thought on the steering wheel last night and was suffering from a mild concussion. Whatever the reason, I was saved from having to recover from my moment as several heads snapped in our direction and Kyle—and me, surprisingly—were hollered at from the bar.

"Kyle! Snowstorm Girl! You're here! Sit with us!"

Stools scraped against the floors as a space was cleared. Kyle and I took a seat at the two that were made empty, sandwiched between George and another man I hadn't met yet.

"You know she has a name, right?"

"Of course I do," George responded gruffly, "But she'll always be Snowstorm Girl to me and probably everyone else who was here last night."

"Celebrating the snow being over?" Kyle asked.

"You could say that. Enjoying a warm meal before I join the fellas again. Should have a lot of roads squared away by morning."

"You're the best," Kyle said appreciably, with a clap on the man's shoulder.

Toni tossed her bar rag over her shoulder and greeted us.

"Nice to see you again Charity!"

"Oh! You know my name!"

"Don't look so surprised," she said with a smirk. "Small town. What can I get you tonight?"

A woman on the other side of Kyle poked her head around him. "If you haven't had a Merry Champmas yet and you like champagne, try that one."

Kyle leaned toward me and whispered in my ear, his hot breath causing a shiver to travel down my spine. "I'm sure it'll be a more mild choice for you; Kerry doesn't drink all that much."

He probably didn't mean to issue a challenge. This wasn't college after all, and I didn't need to prove myself, least of all through drinking. And yet, I turned my head toward him, startling us both at how close it brought our lips. His gaze flicked to my mouth then back up, and while the movement and our proximity caused a response that took me by surprise, I didn't let it show.

"Kyle, what's that drink I had last night?" I said loud and clear.

"Gin—" he cleared his throat and leaned back, putting some space between us. "Gin-gle Bell Rock."

I smiled brightly at him, "That's what I want."

"Ooo-wee" I heard George guffaw. "That's gotta be Toni's strongest. It'll jingle your bells alright!"

"Perfect," I said, giving Kyle a wink.

It felt like we'd been doing a dance on the edge of flirtation since the moment we met. Kyle seemed to be walking closest to that edge, while I cautiously observed from a few feet away, and he seemed to take serious amusement from my reactions. But with this most recent interaction, small as it may have been, it felt like *I* was the one dancing on the edge, and it made me feel more like the CEO I actually was.

Toni set our drinks in front of us, giving Kyle whatever his usual must be since I never heard him order, and I lifted mine up.

"Well Kyle, here's to our one day anniversary!"

He shook his head, clearly pulling himself back together. He lifted his glass, shifted toward me—causing his leg to rest firmly against mine—and we clinked our drinks together. I took a large sip, careful not to show any reaction this time at the strength of the drink, then raised it again and turned toward George, Toni, and back over to Kyle.

"And here's to day one as Snowstorm Girl, getting to know some the kindest people, and actually having time to relax!"

"Here here!"

The rest of the bar's occupants lifted their glasses, and we all took a drink.

"Something tells me this won't be the last toast you make this evening . . . " Kyle muttered, amused.

15

Someone was shining a light in my eyes. I squeezed them shut, then covered them with my hand to keep out the glow.

"Knock it off," I said but got no answer in reply. I removed my hand and slowly opened first one eye, then the other. Not a flashlight—sunlight. The *brightest* sunlight.

I sat up, tossed back the festive comforter, and brought my feet to the ground. I paused when I noticed my attire: I was still wearing my outfit from the day before, plus an unfamiliar evergreen-colored sweatshirt. I lifted the collar to my nose and inhaled, which immediately told me who it belonged to.

Kyle.

I frowned, trying to recall all that happened the night before. There'd been food. Delicious food. I remembered raving about it, but what had I ordered?? There'd been more Gin-gle Bell Rocks. Lots of laughter. . . . and a shot or two.

"Oh god," I said, bringing a hand to my forehead. When was the last time I'd taken a shot? A few times in college . . . perhaps at a couple of high school parties before my dad passed away. It wasn't typically something I opted for, but I vaguely recalled being the one to suggest them after someone—a woman behind the bar, but it wasn't Toni—mentioned a delicious Christmas concoction Toni created.

And what about Kyle's sweatshirt?! I picked up the glass of water conveniently placed next to my bed alongside a bottle of aspirin and wracked my brain some more as I downed the latter with a large gulp of the former.

When we finally got around to leaving, I remembered remarking on how empty the dining area was. The bar was still full of occupants, but

Toni was shooing us all home. That meant it had to have been, what? Midnight? One? When did a bar in a small town like this typically close?

I remembered the steady press of Kyle's leg against mine. Lots of joking. Flirting?

Our group grew to include Kerry and George and another couple, his friend Jack and wife Diane. I remembered cooing over what an adorable pair they made. And yes, I'd absolutely commented on the names. In fact . . . I remembered the bar breaking out in song. A song *I'd* started.

Two American kids growing up in the heartland . . .

An acoustic version had been their wedding song, and I remembered wishing I'd been the one to plan it for them, to which the conversation turned for a time to my company. Did I offer to plan the wedding for someone else who was there?!

The temperature dropped. When I'd gotten in Kyle's truck, I'd complained about it as we pulled out of the parking lot. Where was my coat? Still hanging inside. Kyle offered to get it. I remembered telling him no, then leaning over to rummage in the back.

"You've got to have something here," I said and pulled up the sweatshirt. "Ah ha!"

I'd placed my hand on his seat's back to push myself into my own again, but I'd paused as our faces lined up in the dark. Like they had at the bar. I'd felt giddy. And brazen. And he was right there, his scent invading my senses. His lips slightly parted. That dimple-smirk present as he watched me, clearly amused. But as I paused there, a breath between us, his smile dropped. And then I'd . . .

"Oh no." I facepalmed my forehead again. I remembered the feel of his lips on mine, the flood of emotion that'd soared through me . . . and the way he'd gently pulled back after only a moment. Much, much too soon.

"Put on that sweatshirt, Ms. Evans. We can't have you catching cold."

I did as he said, but remembered pouting. Actually pouting! I'd crossed my hands in front of my chest and stared out the window. But my eyes started to grow heavy as we drove. My head dipped forward, then jerked back up. The last thing I remembered was Kyle's voice: "come here." His hand gently tugging on my arm. My head coming to rest on his shoulder.

"Oh. My. God."

I stood and walked to the window where that extra-bright light was streaming in. I pulled the curtains further apart, opened the blinds, and realized the cause wasn't just sun, but sun reflecting off snow. The scene was positively breathtaking: the backyard was untouched, and the sun set the snow to sparkling. It was a world of diamond dust, and I felt completely different about the scene in front of me than I did when I was driving in it. The sky was a beautiful, pale blue, with just a few white clouds edged in gray hinting at the storm that had been here.

But the lovely view wasn't enough to make me forget the mortification I felt at my behavior. Maybe it was all a dream? Maybe we'd come home after delivering cookies and I'd fallen asleep? I desperately wanted that to be the case, but knew it wasn't the truth. And as I thought about the events of the night before, it almost felt like I was recalling the fun someone *else* had. It was so decidedly not me. That is . . . it almost felt like a parallel me. Someone who might have been if I hadn't chosen my practical, stay-in-control, take charge mentality. Last night's behavior felt so carefree. And a bit reckless, to be honest. Surely they were two people who couldn't exist together. I needed to get my life back on track.

I took a shower, as much to clear my head as clean myself, and headed downstairs, leaving my hair wet to fend for itself.

I found Mary sitting in the kitchen.

"Good morning, Mary."

"Hello darling, did you sleep well?"

"I slept . . . deeply," I said with an embarrassed laugh. "And late. Again."

"There's no need for a schedule while you're here, Charity. I'd relish it if I was you!"

She had a point. When's the last time I didn't have a list to check off? Although technically I *did* have a list, albeit a much more festive one than I was typically used to. It also lacked the urgency I usually placed on myself. What was the deadline, even? Christmas? New Year's? Whenever I drove out of town? And why did the thought of that last event leave me with a sinking feeling?

"Would you like some coffee?"

"Desperately. Is Kyle around this morning?"

"Oh, he's in the barn! And I have a feeling I know why, which I'm positively thrilled about." She grinned, but offered no more details. "He already cleared a path this morning so if you feel up for a morning walk, you can head on back. Actually, he's probably due for a refill. How about I make you both a coffee?"

"Uh . . . sure. What's he doing in a barn? Do you have animals?"

"Oh, no no. But you have to see for yourself."

"Ookay . . .

I put on my boots while Mary poured brew into mugs, put in Kyle's preferred additions, and added cream like I requested. I went to reach for my coat before once again remembering it still hung in The Hearth. I'd brought Kyle's sweatshirt down to return it to him, but with a lack of anything else to wear, I put it on again, inhaling a little extra as it went over my head. Why did he have to smell so darn good?

Mary opened the sliding door to the back and motioned me out.

"Just follow the path," she directed.

Said path wove its way through the backyard and into a copse of trees. The cold air felt refreshing this morning, and I once again marveled at the way the world sparkled. Birds chirped happily, and I caught sight of that cardinal again—at least, I liked thinking it was the same—as it flew from a tree to the feeder, where other birds already gathered.

Aside from their chirping and the crunch of my steps, the world felt extra quiet and peaceful. So peaceful. My embarrassment over last night's behavior receded while I walked, and the memory of a similar stroll with my family took the forefront. It arrived so steady and so strong it stole my breath, and I felt my heart clench. We'd gone sledding on a hill in our neighborhood. Both my parents had joined in on the fun: mom holding Caleb, dad sitting with me. We'd laughed and laughed as we slid down, walked back up, and repeated until we were too tired to trek to the top again, and instead collapsed in the snow and made angels. On the way home, dad carried me on his back. Canned tomato soup and grilled cheese with those individual-wrapped cheese slices was on the menu at the house, plus hot cocoa from the packet. I remember thinking it was the most delicious meal in the world.

My chest tightened and I suddenly felt like crying. I stopped walking and took my phone from my pocket.

Me: Hi Mom, thinking of you. Can you talk later?

I hit send before I could change my mind, then used my phone's camera to snap a picture of the winter wonderland that surrounded me and sent it to my brother.

Me: Doesn't this remind you of winter in Ohio?

I felt nervous sending them. What if they didn't respond? What if they were mad at me for being so MIA? And yet, reaching out also left me feeling a little bit lighter.

I continued my walk through the trees until a barn came into view where they opened up. It wasn't an old barn, or, if it was, the exterior had been completely renovated. It was an unpainted wood, new enough to maintain it's yellow hue, which stood out brightly against the snow. There were windows throughout, but they looked like something you'd find on a house, not ones animals might poke their heads out of. The same could be said for the door I approached: it wasn't a double barn door, but a beautiful sage green one, with metal hardware and 3/4 glass that let me peek inside. And what I saw was breathtaking; the building was totally finished—it was a barn in name only.

Through the glass I saw wide open space with wood floors laden with rugs, a seating area with a giant L-shaped sectional and a small kitchen area. There was a ladder leading up to what appeared to be a loft, and an abundance of natural light, plants scattered about, and a variety of art on the walls.

After taking stock of the place and how amazing it was, the next thing I took note of was Kyle. He looked devilishly handsome in a pair of dark jeans and a gray sweater, hair slightly mussed. He still wore his boots, and a jacket on top of the sweater, and between the two he had on an apron. Not his baking one from the day before, but an artist's apron, covered in colorful smudges.

He was painting.

16

I knocked on the door. I didn't want him to turn and find me staring like a creep, but I was slightly apprehensive considering what I remembered from the night before; was there more I hadn't recalled? The thought made me nervous.

Kyle turned and grinned when he caught sight of me, making my heart jolt.

"Are you painting?!" I asked the obvious as soon as he opened the door. I couldn't help myself. The images on my Christmas list came to mind, and I remembered how he said he hadn't been painting much lately. I remembered Mary was displeased at whatever the reason for the break, so I understood her grin now, and found myself feeling giddy as well. "You're painting!"

He looked pleased at my reaction, opened the door wider and gestured for me to enter with a hand still holding a paintbrush. "It would appear I am."

"I'm so excited! This is for you," I said, holding out the coffee.

"Just what I needed," he said as he took it from me. "It looks good on you. Really brings out the color of your eyes."

"What?"

He nodded toward the sweatshirt and I felt my cheeks redden."Oh. Hah! Right. Thanks. I brought it to give it back to you, but my coat . . . " I trailed off, and wondered whether to bring up more about the night. I decided I wasn't quite ready yet.

"So, you've found my hideout."

"This place is amazing! This is where you live?" I stepped inside so he could close the door behind me. The place smelled like paint and coffee—and Kyle.

"Thank you," he said, obviously proud. "And yes. Well, sort of. I've been renovating it for a few years, but I took a little hiatus because I thought I was leaving, and then I wasn't painting, so . . . " he shrugged. "It's not 100 percent, it still needs heat and a few other things."

I walked to the living space and ran my fingers along the back of the buttery-soft brown leather sofa. "You were going to leave? . . . Wait."

Realization dawned as his words registered. "You've been sleeping out here with no heat?? How? Why??"

He gave me a sheepish smile. "Well I've got a couple space heaters. I use one in the loft at night, so it's not too bad. You made it pretty clear when we met you weren't going home with me, so I made sure you didn't."

"Oh my God, Kyle! I don't want you sleeping out here in the cold!" I was both shocked and surprised that my words led him to do this. Maybe to some it'd be considered a small thing, or expected even, but to me it felt oh-so-thoughtful and charming—like much of what Kyle Morrison did. "Please promise me you'll come back to the house tonight? Where it's WARM."

Kyle put down the paintbrush and came up beside me. "I suppose. If that's what you really want."

"It is," I said, certain. And, admittedly, the thought of him being just a wall or two away at night sent a thrill through me. I started to wonder what he slept in, then moved suddenly to put some space between us and gazed out one of the giant windows to clear my thoughts. "So why were you going to leave?"

I dared a glance at him as I inquired. He'd turned and was now leaning against the back of the sofa.

"I'd like to say it was for some impressive motive like self-discovery or professional growth, but the truth is it was for a woman."

I nodded. I had a feeling that'd be his answer, even before I'd asked the question. "The one who made you stop painting?"

"The one and the same."

"We don't have to talk about it if you don't want to," I assured him, remembering the way he'd reacted to Mary's comment.

"If you'd asked me maybe a month or so ago, I would have said 'no way in hell.' Heck I even bristled as my mom's mention as I'm sure you noticed." He took a sip of coffee. "But now isn't then. I'm more ashamed than anything now, honestly. That's why I wanted mom to let it go. It's embarrassing."

I returned to the sofa, feelings be damned, and mirrored his pose beside him to give him my full attention. "What do you have to be embarrassed of?"

"Letting her get to me like I did. I lost sight of who I am and what's important. Healthy relationships aren't about that; they're about helping you become the best version of yourself—not the best version of the person they want you to be. She did the latter. She wanted to take this small town guy and turn him into the perfect professional: to pull me out of the woods and into the city. I work in real estate. Not sure if I mentioned that before. She wanted me to move where there'd be more opportunities. More dollar signs in a bigger real estate pond."

I thought about my own life in the city as he said this, and realized the feelings that were quickly cropping up for him—or desire, at least, I wasn't quite sure which it was just yet—were dangerous, and not only because that desire didn't feel as controllable as it did with Darren. I realized I didn't want to hurt this guy, who'd been nothing but kind to me since we'd met. And isn't that what would happen if anything took place between us? Because my stop in Auburn Falls was temporary. A layover en route to my destination.

"You don't like the city then?"

"Oh, it's fine for visiting. But I need my wide open spaces. I love the community here. The way we all look out for each other. But do I even need those reasons if the place just *feels* right?"

"I mean, I'm a list person, myself, so a list of reasons sounds about right."

"Oh, are you? I had no idea." He said in mock surprise.

I rolled my eyes. "I am. So I'm not really one to say as long as it 'feels right,' but I understand what you mean."

"Hold this for a sec?" he said as he held his coffee cup out. I took it, and in an impressive move of agility he placed his hands on the back of the sofa, jumped, and swung his legs over so he was sitting on the cushions the right way. He placed his feet on the coffee table and leaned back in a relaxed pose that would make it all-too-easy to snuggle up against him. Damnit. I really needed to get control of my thoughts—they were so wayward here.

"Well that was unnecessary," I said as I looked at him pointedly and walked *around* the sofa to take a seat. I handed back his coffee.

"See, that's the thing, Ms. Evans, you need more unnecessary in your life."

"Oh do I now?"

"Seems to me you focus a bit too much on checking off life's requirements, when it's the unnecessary that gives it true meaning. Just ask C.S. Lewis."

"Who?"

He looked at me like I'd sprouted a second head. "I'm going to pretend you didn't just say that and continue as though you already know he's a famous author. He wrote in his book *The Four Loves* that 'friendship is unnecessary, like philosophy, like art. . . It has no survival value; rather it is one of those things that give value to survival.' Embrace the unnecessary, Cherry."

"You and your mom are quite the philosophers. Is your sister the same?"

"You tell me: what did you think about her last night?"

"Last nigh . . .? Oh my god. I met your sister?! And I FORGOT?!"

More snippets flashed. I remembered a joyful laugh. Someone asking for info on the Hannigans. Sparkling eyes that matched Kyle's. Oh no.

Kyle chuckled. "You're changing the subject. I'm adding 'excellent at diverting attention' to my mental list of characteristics. You don't like talking about yourself much, do you?"

I let out a nervous laugh. "Me? No, it's not that, it's just . . . it's more about keeping a safe distance, I guess."

"From?"

I shrugged, then thought about how he'd chosen to open up about his ex. I decided, for once, to open up in return. "I became an event planner because my dad died."

"I'm sorry, what? These topic jumps are getting way too drastic."

I let my gaze travel past him, out one of the giant windows and across the world of white again.

"It ties together, promise. The lack of control I felt because of everything going on at home when he got sick led me to find and focus on the things I *could* control. That started my obsession with organization. Then I held a successful lemonade stand to raise money for cancer research, which you could say was my first foray into running a business. Then, when he died, well, obviously my mom was a mess. She could barely function. His death made it feel like the world should stand still. Like time should have frozen, you know?"

Kyle was giving me his full attention. And when he nodded in understanding, there was comfort in the knowledge he truly did know, even if it was tinged with sadness at the fact he'd lost his dad young, too.

"But it didn't. I swear to God the second those squiggles disappeared from the monitor the questions started. There was no time to catch a breath, just boom: he's dead, now what do we do about it? My mom couldn't handle it, so I did it for her. I helped make arrangements, I planned the funeral and reception. I threw myself into the process and at the end, well, it was a damn fine event. I got so many compliments, which at the time felt a bit fucked up since we were there because he was dead. But afterwords the statements stuck. And when I really thought about it I realized I enjoyed the rush of it all: the list making, the decisions, the satisfaction when it all came together . . . " I shrugged. "So that's when I knew. I wanted to be an event planner, I don't like things I can't control, and . . . "

I trailed off and swallowed the lump in my throat, not quite able to get out the last bit. *Keep your distance to keep away the hurt.*

Kyle reached over and took hold of my free hand.

"Thank you for sharing," he said as he gave it a squeeze, then moved to tuck a piece of wayward hair behind my ear. "But you know . . . you call it control, I call it fear. And I'm not saying that fear's not warranted, because it absolutely is, but you've gotta let people in, Charity. That's part of what life's all about. Let *me* in, if you'd like. I'm right here."

I swallowed, idly acknowledging he was probably right, and the gentle comfort and wisdom he offered threatened to set loose some tears.

I stood up abruptly instead. "Anyway, that's enough of that. Will you show me your work?"

"If you're really interested," he answered, and I was grateful for the way he let me switch topics yet again without giving me a hard time. He was being gentle with me. It was new, and while it was a little unnerving, it was also appreciated. It felt . . . nice.

I stared at him seriously. "I wouldn't have asked if I wasn't."

"No," he said, looking at me with a contemplative gaze. "I don't think you would have."

He stood, and I followed him to the canvas he'd been working on. I thought I knew what to expect from the sweet images he'd put on my Christmas list, but his skill extended far beyond that. While only partially filled with paint, I could see the pencil on the canvas and knew the direction he was headed: it was a winter scene of contrasts. Snow white with a red barn and a bird in a tree. Quintessential New

England.

"This is stunning, Kyle. The bird. Is it a cardinal?"

He smiled, apparently pleased at my observation. "I was inspired this morning. From watching you yesterday, actually."

I turned to look at him.

"Watching me?" I said, more breathlessly than I'd intended.

"The way the cardinal mesmerized you—it mesmerized *me*. It reminded me there's beauty worth capturing in the every day, no matter what my ex might say. A cardinal among snow can be as striking as a bowl of diamonds, or whatever it is she'd deem subject-worthy," he said with a shrug. "I'd gotten it in my head I needed my art to consist of these extravagant, earth-shattering scenes to make the effort worth it. Leftover from Kelly, I guess. That was always her thing: bigger, brighter, better. Mom thinks I stopped making art because of what she'd said—how I should move on to more serious pursuits and leave the art to the masters—and maybe there's a bit of truth there, but it was more that I just didn't know what to paint anymore."

"What a pretentious bitch," I couldn't help but say. "Sorry."

The idea of someone insulting this man—this kind, hardworking, artistic man—made my blood boil. Although, were the two of us so very different? I was a city girl always pushing for the next goalpost, wasn't I? Hadn't I, although I never really realized it, been stifling Darren this whole time like she had Kyle? Or maybe I was kidding myself, and I knew exactly what I'd been doing, molding him to fit the life I thought—I mean, I *knew*—I wanted.

Kyle must have noticed a change in my mood, because in the next instant, his fingers were gently on my chin, turning my face upward and sending a jolt through me at the contact.

"What's wrong, Cherry?"

"Nothing . . . "

"I can see it's something. I know you don't really have a reason to trust me when I say this, but I want to know what you're thinking. What you're feeling. I'm not just asking questions for polite conversation's sake. The two of us have already done so well sharing this morning, I think. What's a bit more?"

"It's just . . . okay." I blew out a breath. "At first I found myself annoyed with this ex of yours, and the way she treated you. But then I started to think about the similarities between us."

I turned and gently leaned against the counter that lined the wall, careful not to upset any of his paints. I crossed my arms in front of my chest.

"My boyfriend broke up with me, you know, the day I got here. I was thinking about his call when I lost control on the ice. He told me there was someone else. We were together for seven years."

"He cheated? I've got no time for anyone who—"

"No, no. Actually, no. That is, unless you count conversations with someone. He's a decent guy and we had a long talk yesterday. It's just that he said some of the same things you did. About being stifled. Not being who he truly is. I thought all this time he didn't care much for the holidays. We typically work straight through, but he was on his way home with this new girl for Christmas. He said he played it down because *I* played it down."

"Did you love him?"

"No." I surprised myself by the speed at which the answer came out. "I mean, yes. That is . . . I thought we were well-suited."

Kyle raised an eyebrow and had the audacity to "tsk" at me. "'Well suited?' Charity, what is this, the Regency Era? You don't have to settle for 'well suited' these days."

I let out a frustrated sigh and crossed my arms.

"You're one to talk, coming to sleep in an unheated barn so as not to upset my *womanly sensibilities*. And maybe finding someone who's 'well suited' is what I want? An even-keeled partner to go through life with. Not someone to set me on fire the way Darren said this new girl did." I felt my emotions rise, and my voice went along for the ride. "Maybe I don't want to be LIT UP. Burned. Turned to ash. That's what strong emotions like that open the door to: soot and smoke. And heartbreak."

Kyle moved in front of me, so close our bodies were almost touching. He raised his hands and brought them to either side of my face. They were warm and steady. I thought about last night. About how I'd drunkenly kissed him only for him to pull away. I'd meant to apologize, yet now I was standing here holding my breath, hoping he was about to kiss me instead.

"It's not as bad as all that, Charity," he said in a soft tone that had me calming down immediately. "I don't think Kelly and you are the same. And respecting your wishes is hardly a Regency trait. If I was trying to channel a man from the era, I'd have gone the rakish route and actually done what I wanted to when I saw . . . well. Nevermind that. I don't think Darren was wrong about you either."

My heart thrummed in my chest as I wondered at the end of his sentence. When he saw *what*? I registered he'd circled back around to Darren's comments, but Darren was *not* who I wanted to be discussing just then.

"I think you want to be lit up the same as anybody else. You're just scared."

I opened my mouth to offer a retort—there were plenty to spew about how this man could mind his own darn beeswax and how fear had nothing to do with it, even if that was a lie and he was absolutely right—but a thumb slid in front of my lips, halting me.

"Ms. Evans, I say this with the utmost respect: shhhh."

Then his thumb moved aside so his lips could take its place, effectively silencing me apart from the breath I inhaled before our lips touched. Kyle brushed his lightly on top of mine, tentatively almost, like he was waiting to see what'd I'd do. It was enough to make my stomach flutter, enough for me to know I wanted more. I raised myself on tip-toes and parted my lips slightly to try and deepen the kiss. He answered. A hand moved from my cheek to the back of my head, holding me steady as we followed each other's cues to create a kiss we both craved. My head began to spin, and those tiny flutters deepened, as he gifted me a kiss I wasn't sure I ever wanted to end.

17

My phone started ringing in my pocket.

I groaned against Kyle's mouth and protested when he started to pull away. But then the ringtone registered. It took a moment, because it'd been so long since I heard the sound, but a gasp escaped when I realized it was "Mama Said" by The Shirelles. I'd heard the '60s song on the radio once—one of those rare times I turned it on because I didn't feel like choosing what to listen to—and decided to make it my mom's individual tone. This, despite being fully aware most people didn't even use musical ringtones anymore and *definitely* didn't pay for them, and despite the fact we rarely called each other.

Mama said there'd be days like this . . .

I felt a rush of excitement that helped temper the simultaneous disappointment at the interrupted kiss. Kyle took a step back, and the space between us made the big open barn feel extra cold now that I'd felt his warmth against me.

"It's my mom," I said in explanation as I pulled the phone from my pocket. "We haven't spoken in a while."

I searched for a look of annoyance, but there was none to be found; he gave an understanding nod and headed back to his canvas to give me some space.

"Mom." I said in greeting as I answered the call and moved toward the door.

"Oh, Cherry Berry! How nice to hear your voice! Are you okay?"

I was surprised and then pleased to hear her use dad's nickname as I stepped outside, and I smiled as the cold kissed my face—though I had to admit I preferred Kyle's version.

"Hey mom, you too. And yes, I'm fine. Where are you?"

"OH! John and I decided on a European cruise this year! We're traveling up the Rhine and will be in Amsterdam for Christmas!"

"That's really great. I'm glad you sound so happy."

I paced back and forth along the snowy path in front of the barn. Insecurities I tried to keep away attempted to creep in. Was I wrong to reach out? Maybe while I'd been waxing nostalgic, she'd been living her best life and I wasn't even a passing thought. I went to nibble on my thumb nail, then quickly brought my hand down and slipped it in a pocket to stem the nervous habit.

"Oh you know John has always been able to make me laugh, love. It's one of the reasons I fell for him! You know in many ways he reminded me . . . well, anywho . . . I'm not as happy as I could be. Not as happy as I would be if I saw you more."

I felt my eyes water. They watered because I knew she meant he reminded her of dad. They watered because she'd said she'd be happy to see me. I don't know what made me question both things, but I did. More often than I cared to admit I wondered if she ever thought of him. Or if she ever thought of *me*. Dad felt like the glue that held us together and without him I thought we were destined to stay apart and go our own separate ways. But maybe that's just what I told myself as an excuse . . .

My breath billowed in front of me and I shivered. I pulled Kyle's sweatshirt tighter around my neck with one hand. "It's good to hear you say you're happy, mom."

"And it's good to hear you, period. What are you doing for Christmas? Working some big event?"

"So, funny story . . . I was supposed to be at an event, no surprise there I'm sure. A pretty big one too: the Hannigan wedding. But I'm actually kind of stranded in this small town. I got stuck in a snowstorm."

"Wait! This is too much information at once! Stranded in a small town! Are you okay?! And THE Hannigans?!"

I laughed, "Yes, I'm fine. And yes, THE Hannigans."

It hit me then, that while my mom and Mary had many differences, there were some similarities too, which was probably why being around her nudged me to reach out to mom. I'd forgotten one of those things was the Hannigan obsession. Although it shouldn't come as a surprise; just about everyone seemed enamored with them, often calling them the "2.0 Kennedys."Of course, getting to know them through the whole event planning process, I kind of wanted to scream "stars—they're just like us!" like the tabloids. Just like us with A LOT more money.

I heard the door to the barn open and close again, and I turned to find Kyle walking toward me with a coat in hand. He held it out and I gratefully slipped one arm inside the cozy sherpa lining, then switched the hand holding my phone and slid the other through.

"Thank you," I mouthed, warmed literally by the jacket and figuratively by his thoughtfulness. He nodded, handed me a pair of gloves, then disappeared around back of the barn.

"You'll have to tell me more about it," mom continued. "Oh, please say we can get together soon. In the New Year?"

She sounded so hopeful. Her voice was breathy and . . . was anxious the right word? I started running through the busy schedule I already had lined up for January, but stopped myself before answering with the usual "I'll have to get back to you" I said to everyone.

"That sounds great, mom."

She let out an excited gasp.

"Oh wonderful!" her voice got a littler quieter as she pulled the phone away from her face, but I heard her yell, "John, we're going to see Charity next month!"

His gruff voice responded, but I couldn't quite make out the words.

"He's so excited Charity, he says he can't wait to talk to you for longer than 30 seconds on a phone."

I swallowed, unable to help the taste of bitterness that rose from the fact I could sit down with John for a chat, but not my dad—that mom was having these adventures with *him* instead of my father. But these were old grievances. Wasn't it time I found a way to let them go?

"Alright, I've gotta go for now, mom. But have fun on your trip, and give me a call once you're back so we can make a plan, okay?"

"Oh I will, Charity. I will." She sounded so darn happy. "Merry Christmas to me!"

I laughed, confused. "What?"

"Well you just gave me the best gift! Knowing I'll get to see you! So Merry Christmas to me! And Merry Christmas to you. I hope being stranded wherever you are means you'll actually have time to enjoy the season this year."

I'd been idly kicking snow with my boots while we chatted, but I looked up then to see Kyle returning with a saw in hand. He wiggled his eyebrows at me and I let out a laugh.

"You know mom, it's been a long time, but I think this year . . . I just might."

"Wonderful, wonderful. I love you Cherry Berry!"

I'd never stop missing the sound of that name coming from my dad's lips, but hearing my mom use the nickname for me . . . well . . . it was nice, all the same, and I was smiling as I ended the call.

"Was that Santa Claus telling you all your Christmas dreams are gonna come true this year? You've got a smile that'd rival the Cheshire Cat's."

"I haven't spoken to my mom in a while. It was just really nice to hear her voice. And you know what?"

"What's that, Ms. Evans?" He placed the saw over his shoulder.

I rolled my eyes, having given up on convincing him to settle on one name over the other—he seemed to mix them up depending on his mood.

"You mentioned I'd inspired you to paint. Well, you and Mary inspired me to call my mom."

He nodded approvingly, "Lookit us, inspiring each other. That's a good sign."

I almost asked "a good sign for what?" but found I was nervous to hear the answer. I let out a breath and pulled the jacket closed around me; my mind threatened to wander back indoors to the kiss we'd shared, but I halted it with a question.

"So um, what's with the saw?"

"Time to check off another item on that list."

"And that would be . . . cutting down a tree?" I guessed hesitantly.

"Excellent deduction skills. That is, unless we'd like to circle back to our earlier conversation about murder documentaries."

I rolled my eyes and gave him a playful shove on the shoulder.

"Come on, then," he said, and we headed off in search of our Tannenbaum.

18

"What are the odds of us finding the sort of tree we'll actually want?" I asked as we tromped through the snow, an excursion that showed us just how much had fallen; in some spots it almost reached my knees. "Also, these boots you selected were a fine choice, but this is some deep frozen H2O, and I can feel it falling inside again."

"Ah I forgot your jeans would be tucked in. Not so with mine. You can follow in my footsteps again if it won't set you off on a rant about independence?"

I shook my head, now certain he wasn't that sort of guy.

"It'll be worth it—promise," he continued. "And then I'll make you hot cocoa to warm up with while we decorate the tree."

"That means three activities in one go! Multitasking. I like it. Although technically we've already had quite a few mugs of hot cocoa so . . ."

"I knew you'd be all about multiple activities at once, but no cheating." He waggled a finger at me. "It only counts toward the list if we do it now that you've actually got the list."

"Fine, fine. Hey, why aren't you wearing any gloves?"

He looked pointedly at my hands, cozy inside a pair of gloves a bit too large.

"Oh! Kyle! I assumed this was an extra pair!"

He shrugged. "Not fully living in the barn, remember? All the rest are in the house."

"Take them back. Your hands must be freezing!"

"No can do," he said as he continued his walk through the snow.

"Councilman Kyle you halt right there!" I ordered sternly.

He paused and turned slowly around, his lips twitching in

amusement. He raised an eyebrow as I tossed one of the gloves through the air.

"Really?" he asked as he held up the item.

"One for each of us. It's only fair."

He shook his head and smirked, but put on the sole glove before he continued walking.

"So when I finish the list, what then?" I paused for a moment, wanting to deliver the next bit in a way that came across light and humorous, even though I was genuinely nervous he might answer seriously. "Do I get to leave? Because at the rate we're going I'll be out of here by this evening."

"You sound like you're a prisoner or something."

"What! No, no, I didn't mean that. Well, that is, my car *is* currently unavailable. So while no prisoner, I *am* kind of trapped."

"Hmmm" was his response, and I wasn't exactly fond of it. It was one of those replies that could mean so many different things.

He continued to trudge through the woods while I attempted to follow in his wake. His strides were longer than mine, and each step was more like a hop behind him.

"I feel like this isn't coming out right. I was just trying to be funny. But maybe there's some truth to it all. Maybe I *should* be on my way soon?"

"You'd leave a lot of upset residents in your wake."

"What do you mean?"

"Last night over a round of Polar Plunges you assured quite a few people you'd be there for Snowmobiles and S'mores. I believe there was also talk of a wedding consult and some event planning assistance."

I froze.

"What's a Polar Plunge?" But even as I asked the question, I started to remember. "Toni's famous shot," I all but groaned.

Kyle let out a laugh. "Toni's favorite shot," he confirmed. "You whipped out some big-shot company card and insisted on a round for the bar."

"Oh man. I did, didn't I? My accountant is gonna wonder at *those* charges. Ok, well, what's Snowmobiles and S'mores?"

"Another annual tradition. We all ride snowmobiles to the field on the other side of Bear Mountain. We have a huge bonfire, roast s'mores . . . everyone usually brings a dish to share too. Toni's wife typically makes her famous Billionaire Bars, and Toni tends to make her Polar Plunges. Although some people prefer the actual polar plunge in the pond, but that's usually later in the night after a few of the former kind have been consumed—alongside some other libations.

"That sounds . . . wild? Entertaining? Wildly entertaining? Possibly dangerous, too."

"You said as much last night. So even *if* your car was ready for you to drive on home, you don't seem like the type to break a bunch of promises. And I'm assuming that's where you'd be headed, since I haven't caught wind of the way to the manor being cleared yet, have you?"

"Hmm. Good point. I haven't." I sent a quick text to Natalie asking for an update.

"Right. So it sounds to me like you've got at least one more night here in good ol' Auburn Falls."

I thought it all over for a moment, but realized there was really no reason for me to rush off. If I couldn't get to Juniper Manor in time for the wedding, which was—I looked at my watch—a little over a day away, then what was the point? Where would I go? Back to my empty apartment to work? I wasn't about to go so far as to say I dreaded that option, I loved what I did, after all, but I had to admit I was enjoying my time here. Besides, there was a list to finish, and I did *not* leave my lists undone.

"Is Snowmobiles and S'mores on the list?" I finally said.

"Well, no. I tried to put things that didn't have a time constraint since I wasn't sure how long you'd be here. I mean . . . I hoped you might be here for it, but I wasn't sure."

My heart fluttered at his admission: *I hoped you might be here for it.* And, since he was facing away from me, I smiled to myself. "Add it to my list so I can check it off afterwards and I'm in."

Kyle turned back toward me with a smile of his own. "So that's it? I just have to put whatever I want in list form for you?"

"Well, I mean, there have to be caveats. I'm not about to do *anything* just because it's on a list. . . . but most things?"

I laughed and Kyle shook his head, clearly amused.

"Are we almost there?" I asked as we continued our forest adventure. "Because all I've seen so far are a bunch of deciduous trees. I'm honestly starting to think the only way we'll find a Christmas tree is if we head back and drive to a—"

"Tree farm?" Kyle finished, spinning around and spreading his arms wide. "Behold!"

I looked behind him and there, on the other side of just a few more trees and a low stone wall covered in snow between the two, were a bunch of rolling hills covered in pine trees of different sizes.

"Welcome to Fuller Tree Farm."

"Is this the back of Mr. Fuller's property with the mulled wine?"

"Very observant. Shall we?"

"Is this trespassing?"

"We've got a longstanding agreement, don't worry. I'm not repeating my candy-thieving days."

"You know, that reminds me. If you don't mind me asking, you mentioned your dad during that story, and your mom said that he died. What happened?"

He climbed over the stone wall, then turned around and held out his hand. "He died a few years ago. Snowmobile accident. It's slippery, careful."

His warning came a second too late, and his calm share about his father's death distracted me; I put my foot down on one of the snow-laden stones only for it to slip out from under me. I gripped Kyle's hand and he tugged me forward so I wouldn't fall backwards. Instead, I tipped over and onto him, and brought us both down into the snow on the other side of the wall.

"Oof," Kyle exclaimed as I landed on top of him. "You've really gotta stop slipping in the snow like this. I'm starting to think you didn't grow up in New England after all."

"I'm SO sorry," I said, immediately aware of our bodies pressed together. I rolled off and quickly stood. Kyle followed suit and laughed good-naturedly.

"I mean, technically I didn't grow up in New England. I'm from Ohio originally."

"No excuse. It still snows there. I told you they were slippery. We better hurry up with this tree before the both of us get hypothermia and have to snuggle naked to keep warm."

My eyes must have gone as wide as saucers, because Kyle smirked and quickly added, "I'm kidding, kidding. Let's get ourselves a tree, shall we?"

❄❄❄

The farm was full of gorgeous options, and thankfully Kyle was there to keep things in perspective—more than once I went to select a tree he said was bound to be too big.

"Everything looks smaller out here with all this room."

He pulled out a tape measure after my fourth selection failed the size check.

"You had this the whole time?!"

"I wanted to let you try things out for yourself, but if we don't pick one soon, I'll have to take back the joke part of the hypothermia joke. Six feet's your goal," he said, tossing me the tool.

I selected one shortly after, and Kyle made quick work cutting it down while I stood by and unabashedly admired his lower half where it stuck out from under the boughs. My fingers went up to brush my lips as my mind wandered to the kiss we shared, but I dropped them quickly when Kyle emerged, right before the tree toppled precisely where he'd meant it to. And it was at that moment a horrifying thought crossed my mind.

"Uh, Kyle?"

"Mmmhmm?" He stood and brushed snow off his pants.

"Do we have to drag the tree back to the house?"

"What if I said 'yes?'"

"I'd say I'm not sure I'm gonna make it. Trudging through all that snow *without* a tree was work enough."

"Personally, I don't think you're giving yourself enough credit. You'd make it," he said confidently. "But we're not gonna have to test that theory today."

As if on cue I heard a rumble, and a truck crested one of the nearby hills and made it's way to us. Mr. Fuller tipped his hat as he got out and helped Kyle load the tree. He deposited us safely back at the house shortly after, where Mary greeted us enthusiastically from the door.

"Oh what a beauty!" she said when she saw our selection. "And a Fraser fir, too! My favorite."

"I know, ma."

"Of course you do," she said fondly, patting Kyle on the cheek as he passed, carrying the tree with Mr. Fuller.

"The stand is set up in the living room," she called after them. "And the hot cocoa's almost ready," she told me with a smile. "Should be just enough time for you to change into some dry clothes."

"Thanks Mary" I couldn't help but look at her a bit different knowing what I now knew about Kyle's dad—her husband. We'd all experienced loss: theirs sudden and tragic, mine slow and agonizing to watch. But it was loss just the same, and yet her outlook was so different from mine. So was Kyle's. I'd read countless books on grief in the aftermath. It was a logical thing to do after all, and so I knew everyone handled grief in their own way and on their own time. Knowing that helped me justify an array of choices I'd made and continued to make for my life, but since being with them, a nagging voice had started up, quietly and incessantly wondering, did those choices still work?

I hung the jacket Kyle gave me on the entryway coat rack and went up to change. I took off his sweatshirt, tossed it on the chair with some of my other clothes and jumped in the shower for a quick rinse and warm up.

I felt a lightness after the exchange with my mom that translated to a festive vibe, so I slipped on the most Christmasy thing I owned: a sparkly red sweater. Back downstairs, I found Kyle and Mary in the living room surrounded by red and white striped storage boxes. They'd started a fire which crackled merrily, and a tray laden with mugs of marshmallow-topped cocoa sat on a side table alongside an array of savory snacks and cookies. Christmas music played in the background, and altogether the scene felt positively postcard-worthy.

I watched for a moment while Kyle and Mary worked together to wrap the tree in lights. They seemed happy and content, but I knew there was grief underneath. Or, at the very least, a tiny, constant ache from missing someone. But despite this, they chose to gather together, to string lights on a fresh cut tree, to laugh over sap-laden hands. To let festivity fill their home. It was the opposite of what I'd done. But couldn't I choose to do the same now? *Shouldn't* I do the same? The idea admittedly scared me. Beautiful memories from my childhood flashed past again, and the heartache that came from knowing they'd never again be moments in the present hit me like a wave. I placed my hand on the back of one of the chairs for support and tried to keep the tears that suddenly threatened from actually falling. No. It hurt too much. That's all choosing closeness ever led to: endless ache. I took a step back, suddenly feeling overwhelm and the urge to disappear back in my room. To hide until I could leave. To pour over business lists and emails. Flowcharts and potential clients.

I started to turn, but froze at the sound of my name.

"Charity! Won't you join us?"

Mary had caught sight of me and gave me a warm smile. Kyle peeked out from behind the tree, the end of a strand of lights draped over his shoulder. He gave me a grin that set my heart fluttering. And just like that, my feelings of angst began to settle. I took a deep breath and instead of running, I took a step into that postcard.

"Yes, I . . . I think I will."

19

"Are you ready?"

"I guess so. I just can't stop admiring our handiwork!" I answered Kyle while gazing at our tree.

Now that the sun set, it filled the living room with a warm glow. Kyle stood behind me, and I found myself wondering if he was close enough for me to lean back and come in contact with his solid chest. Or, what it'd feel like if he stepped forward and wrapped his arms around me.

"I forgot how much fun it is to decorate one," I said, trying to shake the images. "And also, real trees are my new favorite thing. There's a pine scented candle I get every year from this store I love on Newbury Street, but it's not the same."

"Wait, what do you mean 'new'? Don't tell me you didn't have a tree growing up . . . "

"Oh, we had a tree alright: one we took down from the attic every December. We created ambiance with candles and hanging those little scented things on the branches."

Kyle slapped a hand to his forehead. "That's not . . . no. Just no."

I turned to him and laughed. "You act like I insulted your mother! I'm pretty sure more people prefer faux trees than you'd probably care to admit."

He groaned. "I don't want to think about that. Also, false! You don't want to know how I'd act if you insulted Mother Mary. But I also don't think you'd ever do such a thing."

"Oh no, definitely not. She's too wonderful for that."

"Why thank you, darling!" Mary said, coming into the living room carrying a giant slow cooker, decked in a puffy winter jacket, hat and gloves.

"Are we ready? Charity, I just know you're going to love this. It's festive and refreshing and just . . . oh it's my favorite!"

I raised an eyebrow. I was having a hard time picturing sweet Mary on a snowmobile, but apparently this was an event she looked forward to every year.

"I've never ridden a snowmobile. I'm kind of nervous!" I admitted while I followed them to the hallway and donned my coat. Mary handed me an extra pair of snow gloves.

"Oh I'm sure you'll be alright. I used to ride with my husband all the time. He's one of the co-founders of the event, you know. Mr. Peterson and him were good friends. A group of them used to ride on the snowmobile trails around here pretty regularly."

I had to wonder at Mary's ability to keep riding after learning the machines were responsible for her husband's death. I had a feeling if it were me I'd curse the sight of them and swear them off completely. Then again, I already knew they'd chosen to cope much differently than I.

"Are we all going on the same snowmobile?" We stepped outside, my legs swishing as I walked from the snow pants Mary lent me. The air was crisp and fresh, and I looked up to see a dusky sky that would soon give way to night. "What a beautiful evening."

"This is nothing," Kyle said with a smirk. "Just you wait. And no, we won't be on the same sled. My mom's boyfriend—"

Mary smacked her son on the shoulder. "He is not my boyfriend, young man!"

"Alright, her beau—"

Mary fixed him with a stern stare.

"Okay, her *friend* Tom will be pulling up any moment to escort her. Which means you're stuck with me," he said, looking quite pleased with the situation as he handed me a helmet. He'd already brought the snowmobile out of the garage, and it sat on the front yard in wait.

"Your chariot," he said, bowing in the direction of the sled.

"The longer I'm with you the more I'm discovering just how corny you are."

He stood up straight. "Is that a bad thing?"

I pursed my lips in contemplation for a moment. He watched me, arms crossed, while I assessed. True, he was quite the shift from sensible Darren—that is, who I *thought of* as sensible Darren—but Kyle's personality was infectious, and I found I rather liked the way his cheer, vivacity, and endless corn made me feel. That is, when I wasn't absolutely anxious and off-kilter at the shift. Kyle went with the flow. Historically, I preferred to mold the riverbank.

"No. No it's not." I finally said.

"Good." A clap of his hands. "Now, let's get this show on the snow!"

The quiet whir of an engine became audible then, and got progressively louder until a headlight appeared in the woods from the direction of the barn. The light bobbed up and down as the machine moved over mounds of snow. It pulled up a moment later.

"Did you grab the chips?" Mary yelled to Kyle as she handed the slow cooker to Tom and got on behind him with an ease that affirmed she'd done this plenty of times before. She settled in her seat and took back the chili she'd made.

Kyle nodded and pointed to the bag attached to the rear of the sled.

"See you there!" she said with a grin before she slid down her visor as they pulled away.

Kyle put on his helmet, took his place at the front, and beckoned for me climb on. I followed suit with the helmet then hesitantly tossed my leg over the sled. It was smaller than the one Mary and Tom rode, and lacked the backrest and handle bars she'd settled herself into. My only option to keep from falling off the rear was to come up against Kyle's back, but I tried to keep a tiny bit of space between us to keep from crowding him.

"Hold on," he said as he turned on the sled. I tentatively grabbed a handful of his jacket but he shook his head, reached his arm behind me and pulled me tighter against him. My butt slid on the seat and my chest crushed against his back. He took my arm and wrapped it around his waist. I got the hint, and brought my other arm around just as he twisted the throttle and we were off.

I hugged him tight as the snowmobile tore through the snow. Initial nerves made me squeeze my eyes shut, but when nothing immediately terrible happened, I slowly opened them to find trees whizzing by as we rode through the woods. The barn passed on our right, and I thought we might be following the same path we'd walked for the tree, but couldn't be sure in the dark.

The question was answered a minute later though—it was a much faster trip when we weren't on foot—as we headed toward an opening in the trees. I remembered the stone wall I'd fallen over just as Kyle steered the machine toward a mound of snow that we went up, and as we crested the top the sled went airborne and we cleared the low wall.

I let out a shriek as my butt lifted off the seat, but I held tight to Kyle, and came down with a thump on the other side. My first thought was to scold him for such a reckless move, but as adrenaline shot through me, I ended up smiling instead. Okay. That was fun.

Now in the tree farm, Kyle skillfully wove his way through the dark shapes. My eyes were definitely open now, and I found I enjoyed the way we moved through the wintry night. It was cold, with wind whipping by, but I barely noticed in all my snow gear, pressed tightly against Kyle's back.

The ride continued for another few minutes, through the other side of the tree farm and another stretch of forest. I could tell we were on a trail, and it wove it's way upward until we broke through another opening and out into a field. In the middle, a giant bonfire blazed in the night, lighting up the people who stood around it. Kyle pulled up at the end of a row of snowmobiles—there were at least two dozen others—and shut off the engine.

"Well?" he asked as we stood and removed our helmets. "How was your first ride?"

He was grinning, and it was impossible for me to act like I hadn't enjoyed myself with him standing in front of me looking like a kid in a candy store. I grinned in return.

"I think I may have a new favorite pastime."

His grin widened, deepening that dimple, and I had the ridiculous urge to kiss it. Instead, I distracted myself by putting the helmet on the sled and unzipping the compartment on the back to pull out the hats he'd stowed earlier along with the bags of chips.

"Come on," Kyle said with excitement as he held out his hand. I took it without hesitation, only to realize after the fact it'd seemed like an impulse move on both our parts. I thought about letting go, but decided against it and let him lead me toward the fire.

Whoops and greetings filled the air as people caught sight of us. Beers were immediately tossed in our direction, which Kyle caught.

"Is this okay?" he asked. "Toni is over there making craft cocktails if you'd like something else."

"This is good for now," I said, and he cracked it open before handing it off.

"No worry about beer before liquor—"

"Never sicker?" we finished in unison and I shook my head as I took a sip. "You know there's no scientific evidence to support that, right? It's the amount, not the order, that determines the likelihood of illness or hangover. Most people believe it's true as a result of personal experience and confirmation bias"

Kyle laughed. "Why am I not surprised that's your reply?"

I shrugged. "Before I turned 21 I'd done some research on how best to avoid an unfavorable outcome from drinking. I did some research and made—"

"A list?"

I rolled my eyes like I was annoyed at his guessing. "Yes, a list."

"What a surprise," Kyle grinned and took a sip from his own drink while I looked around, amazed at the setup. I'd imagined a field with a fire and not much else, and while the field and fire aspect were indeed present, there was also a lot more. Several tables were arranged with lights strung behind them between long poles. One of the tables was laden with food, while the other was filled with beverages. Toni stood behind the latter, decked in a blinking headband with antlers. People surrounded the fire, their faces illuminated with a red glow, but there were several groups elsewhere as well. Kids ran around in the dark with glow sticks on their necks and arms or sticking out from various pockets. Older kids—teens probably—mingled together, hovering by the food or off to the sides in conversation. I caught sight of Mary near the blaze with whom I assumed was Tom. I'd been unable to get a good look at him before with his helmet on.

"Is that Tom?"

"The one and the same," Kyle confirmed.

All the faces I'd seen since arriving were there: Lottie, George, Paul —plus more that looked familiar but whose names I couldn't quite remember.

"Ouh, turn this one up!" someone shouted, and in the next instant the Christmas music grew louder, and the singer's voice echoed across the field, accompanied by many of the residents', including Kyle. I'd never heard the song before, but as he looked at me and wiggled his eyebrows while he sang, I had a feeling he wasn't just talking about baked goods.

I sure do like your Christmas cookies baby . . .

I burst out laughing, and when one of the town's old timers approached and held out his hand, I placed mine on top. He tugged me closer to the fire and spun me around, and I heard Kyle holler: "Welcome to Auburn Falls' annual Snowmobiles and S'mores!"

20

I'd been to my fair share of events. After all, I planned the darn things down to a T and prided myself on the fact I'd lost count of how many carried on until the early hours of the morning. But Snowmobiles and S'mores was rapidly rising my "favorite events" list. The food was plentiful, the drinks ever-flowing, the fun never-ending. The town's community focus was apparent not only because of the festivities, but the jar passed around to collect donations for a fund providing gifts, food, and more to area residents in need. I now understood why Kyle suggested I bring cash if I had any on hand, and was glad I'd listened despite wondering what I could possibly consider purchasing in the middle of a field.

As the night progressed, the number of guests and snowmobiles dwindled as families rode home with their kids after time spent eating and playing; the snow surrounding the fire was filled with remnants of their fun in the form of snow angels, leftover snow balls, the beginnings of forts, and snowmen. But for some of us, the fun continued. Jokes and stories were shared around the fire even after the s'mores were finished. I did a lot of listening, not always having something to contribute being from out of town, but even that was enjoyable. And despite being fondly called "city girl" or "Snowstorm Girl" every now and then, no one left me to feel like an outsider. Instead, they welcomed me—sometimes literally—with open arms.

Toni came up with a tray full of tiny shot glasses filled with something suspiciously familiar. "Polar Plunge, Snowstorm Girl?"

"Oh god, not those again!" I laughed, making Toni look slightly affronted.

"Antoinette Gallagher, I told you she wasn't gonna be ready for another," a woman came up beside her and slinked an arm around her waist.

Toni narrowed her eyes. "Call me Antoinette again and see what happens."

The woman, who also looked vaguely familiar, laughed and planted a kiss on Toni's cheek. "But what if I like it when you get angry?"

"Shhhhh," Toni replied with a smirk that said she was actually a fan of the banter.

I wagged a finger at the newcomer. "We've met before, haven't we."

Toni and the woman looked at each other and laughed. "This is Rachel. She's chef at The Hearth."

"Known more commonly as Toni's wife."

"That's a falsehood: *I'm* more likely to be known as 'Rachel's wife.' She's excellent at what she does. I just hope she never realizes how talented she is; she might up and leave and end up at some swanky city place."

I gasped as recollection hit me, and the memory of a flood of flavors came rushing back. "The chef. THE RAVIOLI! Sweet potato with a sage butter sauce, right?" I let out a moan. "Oh my god, they were so good!"

"I know. You told me several times." Rachel smiled with pride.

"Not just Rachel but the entire bar actually—you wanted to order a round of raviolis for everyone," Toni added.

"But we got you to settle on—"

"A round of drinks!" I finished.

"Exactly," the two of them said together, then laughed.

"So you really don't want one?" Toni asked, widening her eyes in a sort of puppy-dog-like expression and waving the tray under my nose.

"Do you have somewhere to be tomorrow?" Kyle inquired, startling me with his sudden approach.

"Oh hello, there you are!"

"Did you miss me?" he grinned.

"Oh, well, I mean, there are so many friendly people here, I barely noticed you were gone . . . "

He'd wandered off earlier and got caught in various conversations, and while it was true part of me wanted him nearby, I also tried to reconcile that with the fact there was no reason for us to hover near each other. Despite the hand-holding on the way in, we weren't a couple. Practically acquaintances, really. Who actually knew quite a bit about each other. Annnd who might have kissed. More than once.

Even so, the way he made me feel wasn't nearly as tempered as Darren and surely, despite some of our prior conversations, I didn't actually want that . . . did I? I remained a mess of emotions as Kyle's grin turned into an adorable pout.

"She's in a mood," Toni laughed. "She cut me to the quick too, and turned down a Polar Plunge after *insisting* last night that I make them."

"I did that?"

The three of them nodded.

"Okay okay, fine!!" I rolled my eyes and took one of the shot glasses off the tray. "And here I thought peer pressure stayed in the teenage era. Who else is with me?"

Kyle, Toni, and Rachel picked up a glass. After an announcement shout from Toni, the rest were quickly claimed.

"Here's to Auburn Falls, all you fine folks, and Snowmobiles and S'mores!"

"Snowmobiles and S'mores!" everyone echoed.

As the drink slid down, I realized why the night before ended the way that it did: the shot was delicious, with just the tiniest flavor at the end hinting at the alcohol it contained. It was like a jolt of holiday cheer.

"Damn Toni, you're good at your job."

"Thank you!" she beamed. "Be back in a bit with another; I've gotta make a batch of Let's Get Toasted!"

"Oh god," I said as she walked off, and put a hand to my forehead. "What is even happening right now . . . "

George was one of the others who'd taken a drink, and I looked over right as he gave a shake like he was amping himself up for something. Then he slipped out of his coat and started unbuttoning his shirt.

"George!" I squeaked. "What are you doing!?"

"If Toni's about to make up her Let's Get Toasted, you know what that means!" he bellowed, which resulted in several other men removing their outerwear as well.

"No, actually, I don't! Kyle!?" I turned to him nervously to find a wicked grin on his face. "I don't know what kind of party this is about to turn into, but I don't think I—"

He grabbed my hand and led me through the crowd which was starting to feature men in various states of undress.

"Come on," he said, laughing.

We walked to the other side of the bonfire and out of its toasty glow into the cold dark of night. We paused about a hundred feet away. A bunch of other people came along with us, and several flashlights were pulled from pockets and used to illuminate the area we faced. Realization dawned as I looked at the dark surface: it was a pond. A majority was covered in ice and snow, but the area in front of us had been cleared away.

"Time for the actual Polar Plunge!" Lottie stepped out from the crowd and addressed everyone. "Just a reminder: this is our last fundraising effort of the year. So let's place our bets and continue to keep our Love Thy Neighbor fund nice and healthy!"

Everyone started talking at once, shouting out various names, and Kyle leaned toward me to explain what was going on.

"We place bets on who we think can stay in the water the longest. They don't have to put their head under, but they have to get up to their shoulders before the time starts ticking. The winner doesn't actually keep any money, though; it goes to the same fund as the rest of the donations collected tonight."

"Do the participants get anything for winning?"

"What is it you said before? The satisfaction of completion . . . " Even in the semi-darkness, I could see his eyes twinkling mischievously.

I gave him a playful shove with my shoulder. "Yeah, yeah."

"They get bragging rights. And also a batch of Rachel's Billionaire Bars. And, depending on who the winner is, some of her brownies, too."

"Why does that depend on who wins?"

"Wellll not everyone likes them. They're a particular sort of brownie."

"Who wouldn't like—" I glanced up at Kyle to find he was giving me a pointed stare. "Oh. OH. Got it. So how come you're not participating, councilman?"

"Who says I'm not?"

He gave me that grin I was starting to love—no, no, *like*—shrugged off his jacket while I stared wide-eyed, and pulled his sweater and the shirt he wore underneath up and over his head. I worked hard to keep from open-mouthed gawking at the sight of his firm chest. His shoes and snow pants went next. As he reached for the button on his jeans, he was sure to make eye contact, and I thought I might combust right on the spot. We were surrounded by a ton of people, yet somehow it seemed like he was undressing just for me.

"Alright, everyone who's participating, come on and line up so we can take final bets and get this plunge party started! The men in town won't be able to find their balls if this takes too long, and then we'll have a lot of disappointed partners," Lottie hollered to laughter all around.

She was making her way through the group with a couple other residents, each of them holding jars with the names of the participants for people to drop money into.

Kyle winked at me and headed to stand with the other competitors —all men—who were standing in various types of swim attire on a board that'd been placed across the ground to keep their feet out of the snow.

I couldn't stop staring at Kyle. He was on full display and I didn't mind the view one bit. I swallowed again. I needed to cool down stat, which gave me an idea. When Lottie got near me, I halted her with a hand on the arm.

"Lottie," I said in an excited whisper. "Is this only for the men in town?"

"Of course not, we just rarely have any women join in. And honestly, most of us take a tiny bit of pleasure watching the fellas freeze their balls off for charity."

"Hmm . . . "

She raised her eyebrows at me. "What'd you have in mind?"

"How about a guest participant this year?"

"Absolutely yes!" she laughed, then headed to the front of the crowd. As she walked off, I briefly wondered what the heck I was doing. This was *the* most unlikely thing for me to do, but what the heck! I liked to think of myself as charitable—it was in my name after all. So it was all for the cause. I started undressing as I heard Lottie goad the guys.

"Gentleman, while I know you're used to one of your bros taking home the win, it's been decided it's time to mix things up. You'll have to stand in the cold just a tad longer, because I have a feeling some bets are about to change."

The guys looked at each other, confused, while Lottie addressed the crowd.

"This year, the Auburn Falls' Polar Plunge is thrilled to announce our guest jumper, Charity Evans!"

There might as well have been a damned spotlight at the event. Flashlights moved in search of me as I walked to the board to stand with the guys in nothing but my underwear. Thank goodness I opted for matching lingerie sets. I kept my eyes on the pond, not daring to look left or right. God forbid I make eye contact with Kyle again. If that happened, I'd probably duck and run.

It's just like a bikini. Fuck, it's cold. It's just like a bikini. Oh my god, so cold. Just like a bikini. What the eff am I doing!? I can do this. This is fine.

I tried to keep my wits about me as I mentally repeated my on-the-spot affirmations. Idly it registered there were hoots and hollers at my participation, and Lottie was yelling about initial bets being non-refundable, so additional ones would need to be made. She was business-minded. I could appreciate that; a woman after my own heart.

"If you're out of cash, grab one of the paper slips and write the amount and your payment app of choice," I heard her say.

Eventually—it was probably just a minute or two, but felt much longer standing in the freezing cold in my freaken underwear among a group of men—Lottie called the betting over.

"While usually you are all out well before the limit, remember: for safety reasons no one is allowed in the water beyond five minutes. Now, gentlemen and Snowstorm Girl, are we ready?!"

I nodded, determined to keep my eyes forward. I'd wrapped my arms around my chest for warmth but refused to jump up and down the way some of the men were.

"You're going down, city girl," I heard one of the others say, and I made the mistake of looking to see who it was. I didn't know him, but Kyle stood beside him, so our eyes met and locked. He gave me a torturously slow smile that made me feel all kinds of things that did *not* have to do with the cold.

"Three . . . two . . . one . . . "

I forced myself to look back toward the dark pond. In the next instant a shot rang out that echoed across the field, and then we were running.

21

The water hit my ankles in a cold shock, and I knew the only thing to do was keep going. If I stopped or slowed, there'd be no getting started again.

Vaguely I heard someone yell, "Oh heck no, it's so much colder this year!"

I rushed forward until the water struck my thighs, then sucked in what little breath I could muster and leaned forward until I was submerged up to my shoulders. The temperature stole the air from my lungs. I gasped in a breath of air, but when my body pushed for me to suck in more—to take a succession of shallow breaths like I heard those around me inhaling—I forced myself to keep it steady. Tips I'd been given during the few therapy sessions I took after last year's panic attack came back to me: counteract fight-or-flight with slow, deep breaths. You can literally lower cortisol production with your breathing.

The crowd was going wild, cheering and laughing as the participants started to retreat. I turned back to see who was left and found myself surprised to find it was just me and two others. And, of course, one of them was Kyle.

"Are you alright?" he asked. He was exhaling in short puffs, and part of me wanted to tell him to slow it down. But I was nothing if not competitive, so I smiled and tried not to break my concentration.

The audience was using various tactics to taunt us: talking about the blaze of the fire, the towels and warm blankets they'd brought for us. The toasted marshmallow shots and hot toddies Toni had in wait. The third opponent swore in defeat and swam to shore and warmer pursuits, but Kyle and I continued to square off.

He was only a few feet in front of me—practically naked—and that realization turned into an unexpected asset. My core warmed as my mind wandered from the pond, taking Kyle and me with it, and deposited us together under a pile of blankets. Our clothes, of course, were left at the bonfire.

"Fuck!" Kyle suddenly exclaimed. He shook his head in disbelief and swam toward the shore. Cheers erupted first for Kyle, and then, even louder for me. I wasn't looking to be a glutton for punishment any longer than necessary, so I swam out just behind him.

Once out of the water, Kyle was wrapped in a towel then a thick blanket. The same awaited me as I got out, although noticing Kyle's eyes were back on me was enough to start the warming process. Were others looking, too? Possibly. Probably? But I didn't care about them. Kyle's gaze was the only one eliciting a response.

The crowd continued their congratulations, and ushered me back to the fire where the other participants were already gathered. Kyle and I took a seat on one of the benches surrounding the flames—close enough for our legs to press together—and gratefully took the steaming mugs someone brought over.

"Not bad, Ms. Evans. What are you, some kind of monk?" Kyle asked in disbelief. "Have you done this before??"

"Hah! Nope! First time." I took a sip of the toddy and moaned happily as the hot liquid made its way down my throat.

"Can you not?"

I looked at Kyle. "What?!"

"You're killin' me."

I batted my eyes. "Mr. Councilman, I have no idea what you're talking about. I'm just trying to warm up and enjoy this delicious beverage."

Kyle rolled his eyes and turned his face forward, which left me to admire his profile and the way the fire flickered in his eyes. My god, I wanted him. I'd been acting like my feels were no big deal—I'd been trying to ignore them and keep it all under wraps. Calm, collected, in control. My Triple C formula. But with Kyle Morrison around all my tried and true methods were flying right out the window.

"Alright, let's get toasted!" Toni cried out, as she appeared in front of us with another tray. Behind her came Rachel with a plate stacked full of what I could only assume were Billionaire Bars, wrapped in plastic wrap and topped with a giant gold bow.

"A round of shots for our participants," Toni said, handing her concoction out to all of us on the benches.

"These are literal marshmallows!" I exclaimed in awe as I picked up the toasted, hollowed-out marshmallow filled with liquid. They must have been toasted in advance of the event, because they were cool and firm, and each was topped with a tiny dollop of whipped cream and crushed graham crackers.

We held out the shots, took back the liquid, then popped the marshmallow in behind it. Toni's description had been apt, but this one tasted decidedly stronger than the Polar Plunge, probably because it was meant to warm us up after our icy excursion.

"Oh my god," I all but moaned again.

"Bourbon and chocolate liqueur," Toni said proudly when I'd finished.

"It's so freaken good," I said. "Total S'more vibes but upgraded."

"Thanks to the bourbon, for sure."

"And now, for our winner: a batch of Billionaire Bars to go along with her bragging rights!" Rachel said, handing me the plate. Then, a little quieter, she added, "Would you like the brownie add-on?"

I laughed and shook my head. "These bars look positively delightful and I wouldn't want to be selfish. I'm sure some of my competitors would appreciate the brownies more than me." I looked down the line of blanketed men to see several hands shoot up.

"A magnanimous winner! What did we do to deserve you?" Rachel smiled as she handed off the plate. "Looks like these are yours to share, gents—a fine consolation prize."

I leaned against the bench and stretched my feet toward the blaze. I tipped my head back and watched the sparks from the fire float toward the sky and disappear; it almost looked like they made it all the way to space.

"It's a beautiful night. Look at those stars."

Kyle looked up then shook his head. "This is nothing. The fire's too bright. You wanna really see some stars?"

"Hmm . . . Yes?" I answered, intrigued.

"Let's get dressed."

Our clothes were brought over during the plunge so they'd stay warm and dry, and we started the somewhat awkward process of getting dressed without losing the blankets that kept us warm. Kyle had an easier go of it than I did: he let the blanket and towel fall to his waist while he sat and pulled his shirt and sweater back on. I tried to keep my face turned away——I wasn't trying to be obvious about my ogling—but when his head was hidden in the sweater I dared a glance at his form. I may not have seen him workout since we'd met, but he definitely did *something* to stay fit. His shoulders looked like the kind you'd want to dig your fingernails int—I shook my head, trying to shoo the distracting thoughts away.

Kyle stood and reached under the blanket. I wasn't sure what he was doing until a moment later, when his swim trunks appeared on the bench beside me.

"Wha . . . what are you . . . "

"They're not dry yet. Are yours? Doesn't make sense to put on dry clothes if what you've got on underneath is all wet."

He put his pants on then, and let the blanket fall away after he'd pulled them over his hips. I caught sight of the two dimples on his lower back right before his sweater fell to cover them, and I wasn't sure what had me more discombobulated: the knowledge he was currently going commando, the sight of so much skin, or the fact I needed to figure out how to get *my* wet underwear off. With other people around. With other nearly-naked men around!

Kyle seemed to sense my conundrum and looked up from tying his boots.

"Want me to hold the blanket up? I mean, or I could take you to Mr. Peterson's house on the snowmobile so you could change inside."

I appreciated his consideration, but didn't want a big fuss being made. And besides, there were stars to see. I stood confidently, I hoped. After all, I *had* just waltzed in front of all these people in my underwear.

"That'd be great," I said as I grabbed my clothes and stepped closer. I handed him the edges of my blanket and he did his best to hold it closed while keeping it loose enough for me to move around inside of. And, to his great credit, he kept his eyes upward, which set me smirking while I dropped my towel and worked to unclasp my bra. Thank goodness I had several layers with me; the cold was certainly keeping things at attention. I hung the damp piece of cloth over the top of the blanket. I knew exactly what I was doing, and perhaps I shouldn't tease him so much, but gosh, it was fun. And it wasn't like he didn't do it in return.

I slipped my sweater on, took off my underwear, pulled on my pants, and quickly scooped up the lingerie. The blanket didn't reach to the ground, and I could only wonder at who saw the switch. No need to leave my undergarments lying in full view. It was easy to justify it when we were all standing around in the same state of undress, focused on the plunge. And charity. Focused on charity. Not me, but like . . . *actual* charity.

"Ok, decent!" I informed Kyle. He let the blanket drop, and I looked up to find more than one pair of eyes trained in the direction of my makeshift changing room—I guess that answered the question about who'd seen.

"Really, guys?!" I laughed, which caused them all to break into action and turn to each other to talk or rise to get dressed themselves. I slipped my feet into my cozy boots after putting the snow pants back on, and we shrugged our arms back into our coats.

"Shall we?" Kyle asked, and I nodded, suddenly wanting very much to be away from the crowd, and pressed against him on the back of that snowmobile again.

We strolled over to the machine, tucked our wet items and my prized bars in the bag on back, donned helmets and gloves and tore off into the night.

I wasn't nearly as nervous this time. I wrapped my arms around his waist and watched as the wintry world sped by. I felt like I was living in the film based off that classic storybook *The Snowman*, when the main character journeys through the woods on a motorcycle at night. There aren't any words, just an instrumental track. And in the scene I was thinking of you see flashes of snow, blurred trees, and the occasional animal scurrying away from the light and sound.

An unexpected wave of emotion rose up as I realized this was the first time I'd thought about the film since I was a little girl; since I'd watched it with my dad. It was one of his favorites.

"Look at all the emotion you can evoke without a single word," I remembered him saying.

I thought about how little control I had over the current situation, zipping through the forest to who knows where with someone else driving. I was a complete 180 from the life of control I'd curated after he'd died. His death left me reeling. I hated the way there was nothing I could do, so from that day on I always—and only—allowed what I could control. The things I could handle.

But not tonight. Not since arriving in this tiny town. It frightened me, and yet a part of me also felt free. Relaxed even. I had someone else at the helm. And I realized in that moment, despite how brief our acquaintance was in the scheme of things, that I trusted Kyle. It seemed somewhat crazy, but that feeling of trust rose up almost as soon as we'd met. I had, after all, gotten in the truck.

The path changed directions, and Kyle now took the snowmobile up, up, and up, until I was sure we couldn't possibly go any higher. We popped out of the woods then, and onto another clearing, smaller than the one with the bonfire and much higher up.

I knew there wouldn't be a single light once Kyle turned off the snowmobile, and that's precisely what he did; he cut the engine and turned the key so the light shut off, and we were cloaked in total darkness, surrounded by silence. We removed our helmets and I looked around, trying to orient myself with any sort of light in the distance—a house, a highway, a city skyline—but there was nothing. No glow on the horizon hinting at far off buildings. Just . . . night.

"Wow, it's pitch black up here."

"Not entirely," he said. "Let your eyes adjust. And look up."

I squeezed them shut for a moment, then opened them again and looked up like he said, and sure enough, stars began to pop out; first just the brightest, then more, and more, and more, until I was sure their numbers would never stop growing.

I let out a gasp.

"I've never seen so many stars! It's so beautiful!"

"I told you to wait," Kyle said, reminding me what he'd told me before we left. "Keep looking and you'll probably be able to see a satellite or shooting star. We stay here long enough we might even catch the space station. "

"You planned this all along."

"I did."

"So certain I'd say yes to coming."

Kyle let out a laugh. "Not certain—especially after your unexpected plunge—but hopeful. And you're worth taking a chance on."

My heart did a happy little flip at his words. "Soo is this on the list?"

"I may have added it earlier today. Call me an optimist. And just so we're clear: you're not allowed to take the list from the kitchen island. I need access to it so I can amend as needed."

"I can handle that. I can't wait to check all this off tomorrow!"

"That really gives you a rush, huh?"

"Mmhmm. The—"

"Satisfaction," he finished. "Oh, I remember."

Did I imagine his voice dropping an octave and taking on a sultry sort of growl? I smirked in the dark.

"Come up front," Kyle calmly requested.

I could have answered with a snarky remark about how I could see the stars just fine where I was, but instead, I swung my leg off the snowmobile and stood. Kyle slid back on the seat, and I settled in front of him, my back against his chest.

"Is this okay?" he asked as he wrapped his arms around me.

I nodded in answer, but the truth was it felt more than okay. We cast our eyes upward and took in the beauty of a cold winter's night.

"You know, I have to wonder, is this appropriate for a Christmas checklist?" I finally said. "I mean, winter, sure. But where's the holiday aspect?"

"Always thinking of the details, I see."

"It's literally my job."

"Fair enough."

He said no more. Instead, the sound of humming broke the silence. Listening to Christmas music was never one of my seasonal requirements, yet it didn't take long to recognize the song.

Oh holy night, the stars are brightly shining . . .

I huffed out a laugh. "Well played, Mr. Morrison. Just like that, our winter's night becomes Christmas carol setting."

Kyle's hands started to move gently up and down my arms as he hummed, and the effect was wandering attention. I stopped focusing on the heavens and thought instead of things much closer in proximity. Like Kyle's body against mine. Like his arms holding me close. Certainly *not* "our dear Savior's birth." I leaned into him more, trying to signal I was okay with his caress. I thought of the kiss in the barn and the teasing we'd done throughout the evening. I couldn't say I'd mind if it progressed to something more—something tangible.

As if in answer, Kyle brought a hand to my chin. Ever so gently, he used his thumb to turn my face to the side. He met me there, and the humming halted as our lips touched. My stomach fluttered, and idly I registered the moment as romantic, an adjective historically reserved for the weddings I planned, but applicable to me more and more in recent days. And all because of a snowstorm, a small town, and a handsome councilman . . .

22

"So, how was last night?"

Kyle gave his mom a questioning look. "You were there . . . "

"Oh no, I was there *earlier*. I know you and Charity went off galavanting in the dark, I heard all about it from Mrs. Meyer at the grocery store this morning."

"You've already been to the store?" I couldn't help but ask, noting the early hour.

"I prefer going at open, less busy that way, especially with the holiday so close. As you saw last night, while downtown is small there are residents spread all throughout this place. There's quite a few of us once we gather."

It was true, I would have pegged the town's population under a hundred going by my first day or two. But then, I should have guessed most people were hibernating until the snow passed, and then had to spend time digging out of their respective homes.

"But you won't distract me from my inquiries!"

Kyle ignored Mary and continued chopping the potatoes she'd placed in front of him. Was that his way of saying the night wasn't as enjoyable for him as it'd been for me? Either way, I decided not to leave Mary hanging or Kyle wondering how *I* felt. We weren't teenagers, despite how he sometimes made me feel.

"It was amazing: he took me for a ride to the top of some nearby mountain, and the view—oh my god. The stars! It felt surreal. Magic, even. That reminds me . . . "

I brought my mocha—another festive insistence by Kyle, which I had to admit was pretty delicious—to the island, took a seat opposite him, and reached for the list.

"You brought her to Landon's Overlook?!"

Kyle's face was down as he focused on the spuds, but there was no hiding the twitch on the side of his mouth. "I did."

Mary nodded in approval, a smug smile on her face. "I'm sure the stars were lovely."

The emphasis she placed on "the stars" left me feeling like she wasn't referring to celestial bodies *at all*. Her phone rang from another room, and she left to retrieve it. Once gone, Kyle looked up and our eyes met across the island—I had a feeling mine were twinkling as mischievously as his. I picked up my coffee and took a sip.

"Magic, ey?"

"Yes." I cleared my throat. "The stars were absolutely sparkling . . . " I added, but I knew he didn't believe me the same way I was skeptical of Mary's star reference.

"Right. The stars." His smirk appeared, and I felt heat creep up my neck.

"So Landon's Overlook is a thing, then?"

"It is. More so in the summer. It's a popular rendezvous spot, if you know what I mean. In school a lot of guys made reference to it."

"Oh did they now? And the reference was . . . ?"

"Well," now it was his turn to clear his throat. "We—I mean, *they*— would just say it's where they were headed if they were trying to stick the landon' . . . "

I almost spat out my mocha. "*They* didn't!" I coupled the word "they" with air quotes.

He looked at me and shrugged sheepishly. "Teenagers."

Our own overlook session lasted until Kyle expressed concern for hypothermia. I'd protested in the dark after he suggested we head down—he made me feel the opposite of cold—but conceded in the end. The temperature definitely dropped since we'd left the party, and what were we going to do, makeout 'til dawn? There certainly wasn't going to be any clothing removal on the wintry mountaintop. I'd already taken them off once that evening, after all. But if we'd been up there in the summer, well, Kyle might not be a teenager anymore, but there's a good to fair chance he'd have been able to crow that phrase to his friends just the same.

Still, I'd held him tighter as we tore through the snow back to the house with a smile stuck on my face. Once home, I was happy he listened to my earlier request and stayed instead of heading to the barn. Our lips and hands found each other again after we removed our things inside, and it was even more enjoyable without a million layers between us. I'd be lying if I said I didn't hope he'd end up in the same bedroom as me, but he deposited me outside my room like a gentleman, and headed off to his own. I realized after the fact, of course, that Mary was just a few doors away, and their old home was hardly soundproof. Kyle Morrison officially had the ability to make me forget all rational thought.

I shook my head as much in amusement at his Landon statement as to clear away thoughts of the night before, which threatened to warm me up more than my mocha. I uncapped a nearby pen and started checking off things we'd already completed: bake and deliver cookies, Snowmobiles and S'mores, visit a tree farm, and decorating. Take a polar plunge and go to Landon's Overlook had been added like he'd said, but the latter was crossed off and replaced with "Oh Holy Night . . . " instead.

"Recent change?" I pointed to the item.

"Gotta be Christmas-oriented right?"

"Right," I agreed as I marked the final box, which he'd made look like tiny gifts by adding a bow on top of each, and took a second to enjoy the rush of satisfaction at seeing the checkmarks.

Mary returned then, a worried expression on her face.

"Aunt June is still sick. Now that the roads are clear I'm going to pay her a visit."

Kyle looked at the vegetables he was chopping and then back at his mom. "That explains the double batch."

"Oh, did I give you enough for a double batch??" She looked over the mountain of veggies she'd given Kyle to chop. "Well, look at that! Serendipity. There's nothing quite like our vegetable soup when you're under the weather, and now you two don't have to worry about dinner, either."

"Isn't Uncle Bob there to take care of her?"

"Oh poo, you know as well as I do Uncle Bob could burn a pot of water. I can't leave my sister to suffer, ill and hungry."

"No, no. Definitely not." Kyle grabbed the chopping board and walked to the stove, beckoning for Mary to follow.

I tried to act engrossed in the Christmas list and scanning the rest of the items, but of course I could hear every word.

"Serendipity my ass, mom" he mumbled.

"Kyle! Watch your language, young man."

"You didn't just decide to go to June's when she called—*if that was even her*—what are you up to?"

"I have no idea what you're referring to," she replied sweetly with a pat on the shoulder. "But now that you mention it, the sexual tension in here is suffocating, Kyle. I need some space."

"MOM!" he hissed back, appalled.

My hand flew to my mouth to keep the snort of surprise that threatened to burst out at bay.

Mary leaned over and kissed him on the cheek. "I'm going to get my things. Don't forget the secret ingredient."

As she waltzed out of the room to the hum of "We Wish You a Merry Christmas," I shook my head. Mary, it seemed, had a bit of spice mixed in with all that sweet.

"You hear all that?" Kyle asked with a glance over his shoulder.

"100 percent."

❄❄❄

I kept saying we weren't teenagers, but my words weren't lining up with my feelings, which seemed *decidedly* teenager-like. As we watched Mary pull away a short while later, laden with half the soup and one of two loaves of sourdough bread she baked that morning, I found myself nervous to be alone with Kyle.

Of course, that's exactly what we'd been last night on top of that mountain, and in his barn, and every time we'd driven in his truck, but this felt different. It felt filled with purpose and expectation. We stood in silence and looked down the snowy drive even after Mary was gone from sight.

I simultaneously felt like I could leap at him to get his hands and mouth on me again, but also like I could run and hide from nerves. I'd lost control of my emotions, which terrified and excited me. I'd worked so hard to keep my feels in check, yet here they were running wild and rampant. I was a professional woman, for crying out loud. But standing next to this man who'd come out of nowhere—well, technically I supposed *I* was the the one who came out of nowhere—I felt completely disarmed. Out of control. Reckless . . .

I decided which of the above actions I was going to go for, and turned to Kyle at the exact moment he'd started to turn toward me. I wondered if desire was written on my face as clearly as it was his, as we took a step closer to each other and—

Our alonetime ended as quick as it started when a truck rumbled up the drive.

"Are you kidding me right now?" Kyle said through gritted teeth, and his annoyance amused me. Granted, I was also a bit disappointed at our short-lived solitude, but when the vehicle pulled to a stop and I saw who was inside, it was impossible for annoyance to stay.

George's burly figure hopped down from the truck. Burly and bear-like, that's how George came across. But teddy bear, not grizzly.

"George," Kyle greeted him with a nod, any trace of his own annoyance gone as well, replaced with an affability befitting a councilman. "To what do we owe the honor of a visit?"

"I wish I could say it was something positive, but Grover's at it again, Kyle."

"What now?"

"I've been in talks with a couple of the smaller towns in the area, and they could use a bit of help with some of the cleanup. Things are pretty well situated here now, you know how great our crew is, but Grover won't authorize assistance. On top of that, I've been telling him we need to place an order for more road salt and he hasn't approved it yet. The storm really brought down our stores, and we've got months to go yet; I think we underestimated our initial purchase. If you remember, I'd asked for more but it was decreased. I hate to bring this to you, I'd like to resolve it on my own, but you know how he can get. I'd been on the phone with him and was so frustrated when it ended, next thing I know, I'm headed in your direction."

Kyle dragged a hand across his face. "Don't worry about it George. I understand, and I'll see what I can do."

George seemed to take stock of me for the first time. "Charity," he nodded. "Nice to see you. Although I have to admit I'm a bit surprised!"

"Hi! Kyle kindly brought me to stay with Mary after that first night."

"Oh the whole town knows *that*, I just meant on account of the clear roads, the tree being gone, and your car squared away at the town garage."

"Wait . . . what?!" I turned to Kyle, who held up his hands.

"I had no idea about the tree *or* your car."

"I told Benji to call you . . . "

Kyle pulled his phone out of his pocket. "That explains it: it's still off from last night."

"Not like you to not have your phone on when so much has been happening . . . " George said, then he looked at me again and realization seemed to dawn. "I mean, not that uh, not that you don't deserve some personal time. In fact it's great to see . . . "

He looked around the drive and I could only assume he was taking note of Mary's missing car.

"Is Mary home?" he asked, confirming my thoughts.

"Ah no, she went to see my aunt."

"Right. Well you know what, why don't you forget I ever came by? I'm sure I can find a way to get around that old grouch. Sorry about all this. I don't want to interrupt your time with Snowstorm Girl."

Kyle put a hand on George's shoulder and gave a squeeze. "It's no problem, I'm sure it'll just take a quick call."

"Don't apologize, George" I added. "This is great news. I'm *so* glad you came by! I need to call my assistant, and then hopefully Kyle will be kind enough to drive me to my car?"

My wheels had started turning and mental lists began forming. I looked at Kyle and smiled, and he dipped his head in answer.

"Well alright then." George nodded too. "This goodbye then?"

"I . . . what?"

"You're about to duck out of town, right?"

"Oh, I . . . " excitement over knowledge my way to the manor was cleared tempered as I thought of leaving town and not seeing these people again. I started to back toward the door. "I do have a responsibility at the manor . . . if I hurry I might actually make the wedding. So . . . yes? Maybe? Let me go make that call. No goodbyes just yet."

Not now, not ever, I thought. I hated goodbyes. I'd rather vanish than utter words which had, to me, such permanence attached.

George nodded in understanding. "Roger that."

I smiled and made eye contact with Kyle to find him wearing an expression that was decidedly *un*Kyle-like. It felt like disappointment and a bit of sadness instead of mischief and mirth. I quickly looked away as guilt threatened to bubble up, and mentally cursed myself for letting my feelings loose. I was once again reminded why it was better to keep a tight rein; they complicated *everything*. I turned to head instead while Kyle continued his conversation with George. Once across the threshold, I closed the door and practically bolted to the kitchen for my phone.

I started pacing through the house. Natalie picked up on the fourth ring again.

"Nat! I just learned the tree's been cleared. My car's in the center of town. I can be there in about three hours."

There was silence on the other end.

"Natalie, what is it? Are you okay?"

"Oh, I'm fine. Great, really. But I have something to tell you."

"Oh no, what happened?"

"Well, you see . . . " Natalie hesitated.

"Spill it!"

"The wedding's off."

23

"What are you talking about?!"

"Sarabeth called off the wedding."

I dropped onto the sofa I'd napped in a couple days ago. Had it really been a couple days? It felt like forever yet no time at all. Natalie's news made me feel like I'd once again plunged into that pond. I tried to follow the same breathing techniques to keep from completely freaking out.

"Okay . . . tell me more."

"I'm not really sure what else to say. All I know is this morning she called the whole thing off. Well, there had been some rumors, but I ignored them. I don't think anyone know's what's going on for sure. I thought maybe it was just cold feet, but her mom confirmed the wedding isn't going to happen."

"Was it something to do with our planning?"

"Oh, no, no. Not at all. In fact Mrs. Hannigan said she was thrilled with how everything turned out, despite her initial reservations about the design choices Sarabeth made."

"That's something at least."

"I'm sorry I wasn't the one to call *you* to share the news. It didn't happen that long ago and honestly I was kind if processing it myself. Sarabeth left as soon as she learned the tree was cleared. What should we do now?"

"It's okay. There was nothing you could do about it. And now, well . . . "

I was about to spell out the answer, but I thought of the conversations I'd had with Kyle and Mary about taking a step back. I thought I'd always be running around and that I'd always *want* to be running around. But I had to admit being in Auburn Falls made me want to sit down every now and then and enjoy a cardinal in the snow or a cup of coffee that wasn't in a travel mug or to-go cup. Natalie already proved she was more than capable, and it was time I leveraged that.

"How do you think we should proceed?"

"Oh! Well, we need to inform the guests there's not going to be a wedding, of course." Natalie answered without hesitation. "But they should continue to use the facilities at their leisure, and enjoy the brunch planned for tomorrow since none of it can be cancelled or refunded."

It was exactly what I'd been planning to say, and I felt pride swell up at what a great job she'd been doing. There was just one thing I wanted to add—

"Of course, I'll have to run it all by Mrs. Hannigan first," Natalie furthered before I could speak, saying precisely what I'd been getting ready to tell her.

"That sounds great Natalie. Really. I can see you've got this all taken care of, so I'm just going to leave you to it, if that's alright. And once you finish up, why don't you take some time off? Enjoy Christmas and the New Year."

"I . . . wait. What? Are you okay Ms. Evans?"

"I'm great Natalie. I've just started to realize success doesn't have to come at the expense of a work-life balance."

"I don't . . . wow. Uh. Are you sure? We won't fall behind?"

"Let's be honest, we both know the benefit gala and New Year's Eve bash always run smooth. We can dive into next year's events at the start of the year."

"Wow. Okay. Yes. That sounds great!"

"Although, we do have several comp tickets for New Year's Eve, so if you'd like to go as a guest, feel free to use some."

"Ohmigosh. Okay. Wow. I'm so excited! This is like, the best Christmas gift! But wait . . . what about you?"

"Well, unless I'm mistaken, it doesn't seem like there's a reason for me to head to the manor; I can see you've got it all handled. Which reminds me, when we regroup in the new year we'll have to discuss your role in the company."

"We will?" I could hear nerves in her voice for the first time since we'd started talking.

"You're so much more than an assistant Natalie, and it's time you were treated as such."

There was a lengthy silence on the other end of the line, and I thought perhaps she'd hung up again.

"Nat? Are you there?"

"Yes. Sorry, yes. I'm just in a bit of disbelief! That is . . . thank you! I look forward to it."

"Well alright then. Merry Christmas Natalie, and thanks for all your hard work."

"Merry Christmas Ms. Evans. Oh! Wait! What about that town you were stranded in? Have you left? Are you going home? Will you and Darren finally celebrate Christmas together?"

"I'm still in Auburn Falls," I said with a smile as I looked at the glowing Christmas tree I'd helped decorate. "And no, no we won't. I actually think I might stick around a little while longer. It's a picture-perfect Christmas town and dare I say I've been having some fun?"

"You?! Ms. Evans, are you sure you didn't hit your head in that crash?"

I laughed and brought a hand to my forehead as I remembered the way it'd hit the steering wheel. "Actually, I totally did!"

"Well if it led you to finally enjoy something outside the office, it might not have been a bad thing."

"Yeah, yeah. Okay, Natalie. I'll see you next year."

As we ended the call, I looked toward the door to find Kyle leaning against the frame, ankles and arms crossed.

"Oh! Hello!" I stood and smiled. "So, in an interesting turn of events, I don't have to rush out of here for work after all. The Hannigan wedding was called off. You heard it here first."

He raised an eyebrow. "Drama. This is exactly the sort of thing my mom and sister would lose their minds over."

I stepped over to him, my heart hammering in my chest.

"Should we go find them to share the news?"

He smiled slowly. "Not just yet. I can think of something else we've got to do first."

Nerves and excited flutters started battling it out inside me. "And that is . . . ?"

He glanced upward, and I followed his gaze to find mistletoe hanging above our heads.

"How about another checklist item?"

"I don't remember 'kiss under mistletoe' being on there . . . ?"

"Don't you?" His dimple flexed. "You'll have to look again."

We took half a step closer to each other.
"That is . . . after, of course."
"Of course," I smiled, just before our lips met.

24

We made our way into town with fingers interlaced. Christmas music filled the truck and I started singing along.

"You're singing Christmas songs now."

"And?"

"That seems new. Feeling extra festive?"

"Well I mean, that was the point of the list wasn't it? Up the cheer level?"

Kyle nodded. "It was. Maximize cheer, minimize stress. You came to town drinking plain lattes, wound up tighter than the girdle of a Baptist preacher's wife at an all-you-can-eat pancake breakfast. And now look at you: cheerful Cherry!"

"Wha . . . WHAT?"

"Oh no, you don't know Golden Girls either!?"

"GOLDEN GIRLS?! Kyle, I'm starting to think you're a grandpa in disguise."

He shrugged, unbothered. "There are worse fates, and worse things to comfort watch when you're sick. What do *you* opt for? A sleazy reality show?"

"When I'm sick, on those rare occasions that occurs, I don't turn on anything. Binge watching shows doesn't help you heal: sleep does."

"Oh Charity," he tsked. "We were doing so well for a minute there. Do I need to drag you back beneath the mistletoe? Or, better yet, the Christmas tree?"

Images flashed, and while I in no way regretted what'd taken place just a short while ago, I was certain my cheeks were changing to match Rudolph's nose.

This was one item I hoped Kyle *wouldn't* add to the Christmas list where Mary could see it, although I was certain she'd be able to guess from the lack of a particular type of tension when she returned. He had indeed added "kiss under mistletoe," prior to our doorway encounter, and I happily checked it off before we changed and left. Another blush threatened to creep up at the memory of our shared shower. It was two times lengthier than my usual wash, and ten times more enjoyable.

"You wouldn't need to drag me . . . I'd go willingly" I finally answered, which made Kyle's head whip in my direction. "Kyle! The road!"

"You want me to watch the road, don't say things like that! Threaten me with a good time and I'll turn this truck right around—"

I laughed and swatted his shoulder playfully. "No! We have things to do!"

A lighthearted groan. "You *always* have things to do."

"Yeah and recently an awful lot of them have involved you, too. Can't say I mind though . . . " I couldn't help but grin.

"Ms. Evans . . . " he warned.

"Alright alright. Another topic. What's with the bothersome Sesame Street character?"

"What? Ah, you must mean Grover. Robert Grover, the longtime town manager and an even longer resident. He's also stuck in the past, my uncle, and an absolute grouch."

"I thought that was Oscar?"

"She knows Sesame Street!"

I shrugged. "I was a child once upon a time . . . "

"Yeah, one who runs lemonade stands! You were born a busy business woman, I'm convinced."

"Whatever. So what's going on with him?"

"Personally I think he should retire. He's given a lot of years to the town, but he's resistant to change, and I don't think he has its best interest in mind anymore. Whether he says 'yes' or 'no' to something often depends on his mood, and these days his mood is typically crotchety. He drops the ball more often than I care to admit, but I can get through to him sometimes, so I end up being the point person for a lot of issues in town."

"Like helping other towns, buying salt, and renovating the café?"

"To name a few."

"Is town manager an elected position?"

"No, he was hired for the role after many years on the council. He has a contract renewed annually, but for the most part it's approved with hardly a glance. The majority of the council—and a lot of residents—feel a sense of gratitude and loyalty toward him. He donated a significant amount of money after he won the lottery years ago. It was used to renovate the manor that became our joint community and senior center, which was dedicated to his late wife. But I've got quite a few concerns about the future of the town and its viability if we don't welcome certain changes. So far, he's been against my suggestions."

Kyle pulled the truck into public works and I immediately found Jackie, free of snow, parked in one of the nearby spots at the adjacent garage. The sight of my car sent a thrill through me, followed by a bit of yearning. It'd be too much for me to go over and hug the vehicle, surely, but it acted as reminder of life outside Auburn Falls. These last few days had been unexpected and wonderful, but I was more than the girl who got stuck in a snowstorm. And the person I was here . . . it wasn't really me, was it? I wasn't a carefree, festive spirit who laughed and played and threw snowballs and rode snowmobiles up mountainsides . . . was I?

So many thoughts in the span of a few moments. I mentally shook them away and focused again on Kyle.

"Sounds like you need to take over the role," I said as we got out. "I feel like you're doing the job without the credit—or pay—right now."

"That's what we've all been saying! But he doesn't want to hurt Uncle Grover's feelings, and isn't confident the town would support him, which is total nonsense."

I jumped at the sound of a female voice behind me, and turned to find a pair of twinkling eyes that matched Kyle's, but in the face of a pretty woman. His sister!

"Emmeline! Hi!"

"Oh, wow, you remember me!" she said as she came in for a hug that caught me off guard. "I wasn't sure you'd remember *anything* about that night."

"She didn—"

"DID after a bit of sleep, coffee, and memory jostling!" I turned and gave Kyle a look then glanced back and forth between the two of them. "Are you two—"

"Twins?" She finished with a grin. "Yep! But I guess you didn't remember *everything* because we definitely had this conversation. Let me repeat the highlights: fraternal not identical, and Kyle was born first by a mere 3 minutes. He loves telling people he has a younger sister."

"Oh come on, you like saying you have an older brother just as much!"

"I do," she said with a grin.

"Anyway, what are you doing here, sis?"

"Well I mean it's my town, too! And isn't it a gorgeous day?!" She spun around for emphasis. "I've been taking some wintry shots of downtown. Pure serendipity we're in the same spot at the same time, *bro*." She leaned toward me like she was about to share a trade secret. "Admittedly, in a town as charming as this serendipity takes place with regularity."

"And by charming she means small," Kyle added as we headed over to Jackie.

I patted her fondly on the trunk. I was thrilled she appeared unharmed from our adventure.

"No, no I mean charming! Wording is everything, Kyle Morrison. As a politician you should know that!"

"Oh I do, I just like annoying you." Kyle turned his attention to me. "Emma, you'll quickly learn, is one of Auburn Falls' biggest fans. She runs a social media account where she shares photos throughout the year."

She let out a dramatic sigh, then took out her phone and, as though to prove her point, took a photo of the public works building.

"What could you have possibly found photoworthy *there?*"

"My dear brother, it's all in how you frame it."

She turned her phone so we could look, and I had to admit, it was a nice shot. She'd framed it off center and included a portion of the brick building with a large window that looked in on a tree decorated with red and white lights. The rest of the photo was a nature shot of the snow-covered hill behind the building, framed by a line of pine trees.

"That's lovely. Oh! Seeing you reminds me: I've some news to share that you might be interested in hearing."

"Tea?!"

Emmeline practically squealed when I nodded.

"Spill it!"

"What?!" Kyle asked, confused.

"Kyle, you're the same age as me, don't act like a grandpa. Gossip!"

"I said he was acting like a grandpa before, too!"

"See?" Emmeline linked her arm through mine. "We're meant to be in Kyle's life so we can torture him equally. Where are you headed?

Shall we take a winter walk?"

I looked over my shoulder at Kyle for some direction, to find he was shaking his head incredulously at his sister. "I have to give George an update, then we were on our way to Clark's. I have . . . plans. For Charity and me. I need a few things."

My stomach fluttered at his words, while Emmeline let out a tinkling laugh.

"Don't worry, I can take a hint. I'm not about to crash your party, mom already warned me not to pop in. Aunt June's not even that sick, you know. We'll meet you at the store."

"Trust me, I know." Kyle said as he headed in the building.

I hoped the cold air had already given my cheeks a rosy hue. The nonchalant way they were talking about the set-up for Kyle and me to be alone was somewhat alarming. I was definitely not used to such candid discussion.

Emmeline and I headed up the sidewalk, our feet crunching on sand, salt, and hardened snow.

"Alright, tell me!"

"Sarabeth called off the wedding!"

"Oh my god, NO!" she gasped and abruptly stopped moving, pulling me to a halt with her. "Do you think the rumors are true then?"

"What rumors?!"

"You're her wedding planner and you don't know the rumors?! They were all over social media when she announced her engagement, and continued to circulate even as the wedding date approached."

Emmeline took out her phone and started browsing.

"I have to admit, if it doesn't relate to my work I'm not typically on social media. I'm an event planner, not a therapist or gossip mill— present share session aside—so no, I didn't hear about any rumors."

"A lot of people think she fell in love with this guy while she was on vacation in the islands and never really got over it. There were a few photos taken. But you know, same old story: pressure from disapproving parents, vacation ended, et cetera."

"Interesting," I mused, and wondered if Natalie had any more insight. Not that it really mattered in the end, my company got paid even without the actual "I do," so whatever led to Sarabeth's decision was none of my business. Even *if* I could admit I was a bit intrigued.

"Have you told my mom yet?"

I shook my head, "She was already gone when I found out."

Now Emmeline squealed for real. "Ouh I can't wait to tell her!"

Our tête-à-tête ended as we walked through the parking lot for Clark's Groceries and were approached by a very pregnant woman with her arms laden with bags.

"Hi Emmeline!" she said, somewhat breathlessly.

"Abigail! What are you doing out here? I thought you were supposed to be on bedrest!"

"Yes, I know. But I was bored. AND the Christmas Eve party is coming up! Can you believe it's already here? And there's still more to do! Paula had the kids from her class help out but I don't trust them for the life of me. If we leave high schoolers in charge of things like decorations God only knows what we'll walk into Wednesday." She turned to me and smiled. "Charity, right? I'd shake your hand but I might drop all this. Nice job winning the Polar Plunge. Jim came home in a bit of a huff, and I laughed hysterically. It's about time someone humbled those men."

"Oh! Thanks!"

"What about me!? Did *I* need to be embarrassed that way?" Kyle approached from behind and my stomach flipped at the sound of his voice.

"I said what I said councilman," Abigail smiled while Kyle narrowed his eyes.

"Does Jim know you're out here prepping for a party?"

She fixed Kyle with a stern stare. "No, and I'm not under house arrest you know!"

"I know that, Abigail, but don't you think he'll be worried about you and those babies?"

She deflated. He'd obviously hit a soft spot.

"Of course he will be. And look, if I'm being honest I'd rather be eating ice cream and enjoying a Christmas movie marathon, but what am I supposed to do? Everyone looks forward to this event all year!"

If we were living in one of the movies she was yearning to watch, I could have been the director. I knew exactly what would happen next. And, sure enough, Kyle, Emmeline, and Abigail turned to me at the same time.

"Charity, what is it you do for work? Jim mentioned some things, but you never can tell what's fact or fiction when stories are circulating at the same time as alcohol. Especially during Snowmobiles and S'mores.

"I own an event planning company out of Boston."

"Oh wow. Oh. Okay. So it's true then. I'm sure working with you is really expensive though . . . you probably book out at least a year in advance."

She wasn't wrong on either account, but I didn't admit as much. "Well actually, believe it or not my schedule is kind of open right now. Would you like me to finish getting everything ready? You know what they say about idle hands. "

"Oh would you!?"

"I don't know that I'd say your hands have been idle, Ms. Evans . . . " Kyle waggled his eyebrows and my stomach fluttered at the insinuation.

"Well, at least as it pertains to event planning." I gave him a pointed look, but I could tell by the glances Abigail passed between us she knew exactly what was going on. I had a feeling I was going to remain the topic of gossip in this town for however long I stayed. "Besides, you said yourself Abigail's supposed to be resting, and Jim will be worried. Also . . . it's a *Christmas* event. Surely this can be added to the list?"

"As you wish," Kyle said with a slight bow.

I caught Emmeline roll her eyes. "Ok Westley."

"Westley?"

"A movie reference. The Princess Bride," Emmeline explained. "Please ignore him."

Kyle smirked at his sister and turned back to Abigail. "Well, you heard the woman. Looks like Satin & Splendor is officially helping with the Auburn Falls' Christmas Eve party."

"Oh la! This is gonna be the fanciest fête we've ever seen!" Abigail exclaimed as she handed us her bags. "Oh wait, not that one! That's my ice cream," she said with a smile as she took one back. "Now, just one more second," she added as she rummaged in her purse. "Ah! Here it is."

She pulled out a crumpled piece of paper and handed it to me. "I'm usually a little more organized than this, but, you know . . . pregnancy brain. Honestly, thanks so much! I can't wait to see how it turns out!"

And with that, Abigail waddled to her car and drove off to enjoy ice cream and Christmas flicks.

"Welp, guess we've got our afternoon scheduled now, don't we?"

"Excuse me—we?" Kyle asked like he was genuinely appalled.

"Of course! I'm a visitor, Mr. Councilman, I don't know enough about this place to do it justice or figure out where to get the things I might need to get it done without your help. I have staff, you know."

I looked at Emmeline.

"Are you in too?"

"Oh, I wish I could, but I don't want to," she said sweetly. "I'm more party *attendee* than party planner. Good luck though!"

I laughed at how forthright she was and decided it had to be a family trait.

"Fair enough."

"Speaking of parties," her brother began, "where were you last night?"

"Ugh. I don't want to talk about it. I said 'yes' to a first date like a fool. It was terrible, so I missed all the fun for nothing. See you later!" she waved over her shoulder as she headed off.

"I like her," I said as I opened Abigail's paper.

"She's alright," Kyle added, nonchalant, but I could already tell they had a great relationship.

"Oh wow." I looked down to find notes scattered all over the page: scrawled tidbits about decorations and food and entertainment. There didn't seem to be any sort of rhyme or reason to what Abigail wrote out, and the sight just about gave me a headache.

"Okay. First things first: I've gotta fix this list. Up for a cinnamon bun?"

25

"You really do love this, don't you?" Kyle asked as I emptied the supplies from Abigail.

This certainly wouldn't be one of my more lavish Christmas Eve events—there was no China or silver to be found—but then, I doubted that's what they'd want anyways. I wasn't about to reinvent the wheel or upset the status quo, so paper plates and plastic utensils it was. At least the plates featured festive designs.

"Is it that obvious?"

"You're emptying grocery bags and grinning, and you were positively giddy as you rewrote the list with those colored pens of yours at Lottie's. You almost let your cinnamon bun get cold, which is basically illegal."

I laughed. "Yes, yes I do."

The part I didn't say aloud was how much it made me itch to get back to my actual work. I loved my company, and while this unexpected time in an unexpected place with an unexpected man I was admittedly getting unexpected feelings for had been enjoyable, it didn't come with a magic spell that made me forget the life I had outside Auburn Falls. Coupled with seeing Jackie and the knowledge the roads were safe enough to drive on again, I couldn't help but wonder when the right time to leave would be. The thought admittedly came alongside a twinge of sadness. Maybe I didn't need to figure it all out just yet. I had a list to finish, after all . . .

"I wish I had a couple days notice; I could have had some decorations shipped 1-day," I mused as I pulled out rolls of streamers and left the rest of my thoughts unsaid.

After organizing Abigail's atrocity of a list we'd moved to the basement of the local congregation where the party was traditionally held. While the town could potentially host it in the community center now thanks to grouchy Grover, prior to the renovation Kyle explained the meeting room was the largest heated space in town. Since it was already equipped with a kitchen and several bathrooms, it made the most sense for indoor functions. There was more room and newer amenities at the community center now, but a town like Auburn Falls was a town that liked tradition.

"Everyone sleeps a little better paying rental fees to the congregation anyways," Kyle mused while he made a cup of church coffee. "Love Thy Neighbor is managed through here, and they do plenty of other ministry for the neighboring communities, too. I think they've come to rely on the rental fees. This and the polar plunge really make an impact. A few years ago church leadership even pushed the Christmas Eve service to an earlier time to avoid conflict. Official Christmas Eve stance is: prayers then party," Kyle smirked.

"The pastor doesn't mind drinking in the church basement?"

"I asked him once before. His response? 'Even Jesus drank wine.'"

"That's fair," I laughed and nodded appreciably. "I just hope I can get it to smell a bit more festive in here."

The space, while not terrible overall, boasted a bit of a musty aroma.

"Oh I'm sure once the food arrives that'll happen."

"Anywhere I can get scented candles to help it along?"

"Oh sure, there's a woman who runs a small candle business out of her home. That is, she mostly makes them for family and friends, but I'm sure she'd be happy to give you some. Just so long as you have plans to keep this firesafe. If you recall, Abigail's husband is a firefighter. I'd like him to be able to enjoy the party, not put out a fire."

"Actually I thought I'd wrap paper cut in the shape of Christmas trees around the jars." I rolled my eyes. "Of course! We can put a row on the top shelf over there, removed from everything else. I was thinking to use the rest of that sideboard for cookies," I said as I added a check next to "scent."

Part of my planning process involved making sure there was something for all the senses, which I always found helped ensure a well-rounded event. Next on the list was sound.

"What about music?"

"This room has built in speakers. We usually just turn on a Christmas playlist."

"Hmm. Well, I suppose that'll have to do considering the short notice. I know Abigail scoffed at high schoolers taking the helm, but since there'll be guests of all ages, the playlist should have something for everyone. I'll pull up a classic Christmas playlist, then we should let them add some of their favorites holiday tunes. Can you call them down?"

"The high school kids?"

"No, Kyle, Santa's elves." I said with a laugh. "YES, the high school kids! Didn't Abigail mention someone who had their students help?"

"Yeah, her sister Paula is an English teacher. But you want me to somehow get a group of high school kids down there . . . to help . . . on a Sunday?"

"I believe in you." I leaned over and kissed him on the cheek.

"I'll see what I can do," Kyle smirked and pulled out his phone. "Hey Paula," he said a moment later. "I'm good, how are you? Great. Hey, so, I'm at the church with Ms. Evans . . . yes. Yes, the one and the same. She's helping with the Christmas Eve party. Yes . . . Alright. . . . Hey do you think there's any way you could convince some of your kids to come by and help? . . . Yeah that'd be great. Okay, thanks."

Kyle put his phone down and fixed me with a smug stare. "And done. She's gonna send a message through their class chat or whatever it is they use these days." He walked over to the table where I was sitting and leaned over me to take a peek at my list. "What's next, boss?"

"Sight."

"What?"

"Decorations."

He held up a roll of red streamer. "Isn't that what this is?"

"That's not going to cut it this year. Not if I'm putting the S&S name on it."

"I mean, it's Auburn Falls. No offense, but I don't think your company is going to get any publicity from this."

"Do you have a phone, councilman?"

"You just saw me use it," he said, taking a seat on the edge of the actual table, a bit too close for comfort. His proximity was distracting, but events were my forte so I pretended I wasn't impacted.

"Do these high school kids have phones?"

"Of course they do. Most of them, anyways."

"Does Mary have a phone?"

"Okay, where are you going with this?"

"You should know geographical location doesn't really matter anymore. Anything can be shared and accessed all around the world—anything can go viral. I've worked hard to curate a specific brand, and I intend to keep it intact."

Kyle frowned. "So you're saying small-town streamers aren't good enough?"

"No, but I'm saying if I'm being brought on to help I'd like to do something different, something that says 'Satin & Splendor was here.'"

Kyle stood and walked toward the coffee station again. I knew for a fact he hadn't finished his other cup, so I could only assume he'd moved that way because he was miffed.

I followed in his wake. "I upset you."

"No."

"Kyle, don't do that. We're not teenagers. Talk to me."

His eyes met mine. "You just hit a nerve."

"Kelly."

"This town was never good enough for her. She talked down just about every aspect. Her 'compliments' were always thinly veiled insults, like 'what a sweet store. If only if offered X." Or 'this event is wonderful, but you know what would really take it over the edge?' That kind of thing. And, as you know, she said the same sort of thing to me."

"I didn't mean to bring up those feels," I said earnestly as I placed a hand on his shoulder. "This town is great as is—and so are you, Kyle, truly. Events just get me excited. I'm always trying to zhuzh 'em up. It's what I do! I'd never try to erase what makes this town so charming. I feel like my stance is the same as yours! What is it you said earlier? The town needs to embrace certain changes? Not erasure, just enhancement."

Kyle nodded in understanding.

"You're absolutely right. Sorry, I just . . . I guess every now and again I let my hope falter. I appreciate you explaining yourself more."

"Communication is key. A skill that requires constant practice."

"Well they do say practice makes perfect . . . " he said quietly, and I didn't think he was talking about communication or the town anymore, especially not when his gaze kept flicking down to my mouth.

I realized then it'd been far too long since we last kissed, as passion for my work stole my focus the moment Abigail handed me the reins. But now . . . oh, now that focus had returned to councilman Kyle and a different sort of passion. I smiled slowly and licked my lips.

"Jesus, Charity . . . "

I was about to tell him not to use the Lord's name in vain—especially not in the basement of a freaken church—but he crushed his lips against mine before I had the chance. And then I didn't care about words or locations, because our hands were on each other again, and memories of earlier filled me with excitement at the thought of making more. My arms linked around his neck while his hands roamed down my back. I could feel him against me and I moaned against his mouth. Oh how I wished there were no fabric layers between us.

He moved away from my lips and I whimpered in protest until he trailed kisses along my jaw, paused to nibble my earlobe—sending shivers down my spine—then swept my hair away from my neck and kissed me there. His actions turned my sound of protest into one that asked for more.

I was breathless, and knew I'd face potential damnation and let him take me then and there if he continued, but maybe we were already cursed, because the metal door at the top of the stairs opened, and teenage voices carried down, separating us so fast you'd think we'd been shocked.

I brought a hand to my mouth to keep from laughing at yet another interruption, but Kyle looked less than pleased.

"If we get interrupted one. More. Time. . . " He said through clenched teeth, which only made a laugh escape that came out more like a snort. "I'm going to revisit that Regency Era talk. I'm suddenly contemplating tossing you over my shoulder and bringing you back to the barn for some isolation."

"You know, that doesn't sound all that bad."

"That's not helping, Ms. Evans."

He let out a huff and turned back to pour himself yet another drink, but I knew this time he was only trying to busy himself until he settled down.

"Hello?!"

"Hi!" I said to the kids as they appeared. "Thanks for coming! Let me show you what I need you to do . . . "

26

A couple hours later, with the afternoon sun low in the winter sky, Kyle and I made our way to the front door of a quaint cottage in the woods, munching the remains of popcorn samples we'd selected for the party. After my focus shifted from Kyle back to planning—that is, as much as it could with him standing nearby—I'd learned from some very enthusiastic teenagers that Auburn Falls had local makers I could leverage for the event.

Carol's Corn was one of them. The kids raved about her delicious popcorn, and after reaching out, she was more than happy to come by with samples. Kyle's favorite was caramel, while mine was white chocolate. Peppermint chocolate would also be available, as well as good ol' salted. A quiet, friendly woman, Carol shyly accepted our praise and happily agreed when I asked her to make the snack into popcorn balls. I planned to suspend them from the ceiling around the edge of the room for an interactive element. They'd be mixed with the paper snowflakes I had the teenagers work on for a snow-like effect.

And, in the end, much to Kyle's amusement, I decided to use some streamers, after all. I skipped the red but used white to make a streamer canopy from the light fixture in the center of the room to the edges. The addition of strands of lights brought the entire thing together, and I was thrilled with how the space transformed.

We'd handled taste via a conversation with Toni and Rachel, whose staff would take care of the buffet per usual with a few suggested tweaks, like a single signature cocktail to go with a selection of beer and wine. Since I was taking inspiration from the Hannigan wedding and opting for a dialed back winter wonderland theme, I suggested a cocktail version of the Polar Plunge shot, rebranded as the Winter

Whiteout.

As per tradition, attendees would also bring their favorite cookie for the display, and I pulled together plans for a hot cocoa table that would look like a winter village I was sure would be a hit with kids and adults alike. Thanks to the presence of a quilting group at the church Carol was conveniently part of, and a member who apparently had an affinity for "puff quilts" whatever those were, I had access to a fluffy fiber fill I could use for pretend snow.

Her neighbor Jessica, Carol shared, also loved Christmas villages so much she had multiple rooms in her home with the items on display. She hosted open house hours throughout the season for people to stop by and enjoy them. Carol was certain there were solid white ones in the mix Jessica would likely let us borrow, and would probably be thrilled to help with the setup, too.

And that was how Kyle and I ended up en route to a Christmas village viewing.

"I'm so impressed with how willing everyone is to help out around here," I mused as we stood on the steps and Kyle rang the bell. "All my help has to be paid!"

"A small town perk I suppose. And you've actually got financial goals to achieve with your events. Around here, we're in it for community."

The door was opened by two little girls, followed close behind by a man and woman.

"Are you here to see the magic village?" one of the girls asked.

"We are!" Kyle replied enthusiastically.

"We've got cocoa for you!" added the other.

"Well doesn't that sound absolutely perfect," he said. And as we were welcomed in and introductions were made, I found myself as enamored with the Sweet family—literally their last name and oh-so-fitting—as I was with the easy way Kyle interacted with their daughters Penny and Olivia.

What followed was a magical trip, led mainly by the girls, through three rooms laden with Christmas village scenes, complete with a working train that made its way up and over the top of one of the door frames. We sipped cocoa, nibbled cookies, and let ourselves get wrapped up in the girls' excitement as they showed us their favorite buildings and vignettes.

"Look close at this one! You can see in the windows at the elves working!"

We bent down and sure enough, inside the small building one elf could be seen sawing back and forth on a piece of wood, while the other lifted and brought down a hammer on a tiny toy.

"That's wonderful!" I said as they tugged Kyle away to look at a mini ice skating rink. "This is quite the labor of love," I told Jessica as I stood up.

"You've no idea," John answered as he wrapped an arm around his wife's shoulders and gave a little squeeze.

"He means because of my sister. Some of these were hers."

The me before Auburn Falls would have nodded and said no more, not wanting to pry or get wrapped up in someone else's business. But now I was an odd mix of the me before and the me now: someone who was opening up—just a tad—and was willing to let others open up in return.

"Were?"

"She died a few years ago. Cancer. But we both collected these. It started with gifts from our grandmother; she'd give us each one for Christmas, and we set them up together as girls, slowly building our little town."

The C-word sent a pang through me. I swallowed hard and nodded.

"I lost my dad to cancer. It's a wonder you put these up at all. Doesn't it hurt?"

"Oh, always and forever. But there's joy, too. There's memory attached to each piece we received together, and it makes me smile taking them out and setting them up every year, even though there's also sadness we won't collect more together."

I nodded and decided she was a stronger woman than I was. I'd opted to keep most of the things that reminded me of my dad in a box.

"I love sharing this with others," Jessica continued. "I know she'd have loved it, too."

"Have you ever contemplated fundraising?"

"For . . . ?"

"Well, it could be in her honor. This is such a lovely thing: opening your home, giving a tour, the hot cocoa . . . you could charge a small admission fee to raise money for cancer research in her honor."

Kyle stepped back beside me and put an arm around my waist, a move that sent a thrill through me.

"Even now she plans events!" he said.

"Sorry, I can't help it! It's what I do."

"That's a great idea, actually." John admitted, just as Jessica gave my arm a gentle squeeze.

"Sorry about your dad."

I gave her my standard don't-worry-about-it smile and turned to Kyle, ideas forming, with no desire to linger on the sad bits of my past.

"You know, this town has such charm. It could easily become a destination, not just a place people pass through like you said the night we met. Unique events like a holiday village tour for charity are the kind of thing people look for these days. I bet there's plenty more opportunities like that hidden around here."

John and Jessica gave each other a look.

"Sounds like she needs to join you on the council," Jessica said, amused. "Maybe she'd have better luck with your uncle."

"Now there's an idea," John added. "Looking to move to town?"

I laughed, even though inside his question set my nerves on high alert. Like Kyle knew exactly what I was feeling, he let go and stepped away, and I missed his warm, sturdy frame immediately.

"Ms. Evans has a life in Boston," he answered for me. I bit my lip. He wasn't wrong, yet my feelings once again felt all sorts of mixed up.

"Would you two like to join us for dinner?" John asked as we finished the tour and Jessica let me choose several pieces for the party.

"Ordinarily I'd say 'absolutely,' but Ms. Evans and I have a date with a Christmas movie this evening."

"We do?"

"It's on the list."

"Oh! The plans you mentioned earlier! What movie are we watching?"

"I'd tell you I was hurt you forgot except quite a bit has happened since we got to town. And I haven't decided yet. That all depends on what you've already seen."

"I'm ashamed to admit the list isn't long. When I was a child I'm sure I watched some with my family. I remember *A Charlie Brown Christmas* for one, and *The Snowman* which I think is somewhat niche, but apart from that . . . " I gave an apologetic shrug.

"*White Christmas*?" Kyle asked.

"Er . . . yes. It looks like it's definitely going to be one."

"No, no. Tell me you've *seen White Christmas*."

I shook my head.

"Alright, that's it. That's what we're watching."

"A solid choice," Jessica affirmed, just as her daughters put their arms around each other's shoulders and started to sing.

"Sisters, sisters . . . never were there such devoted sisters!"

It was an adorable sight, even if I was unsure what they were doing.

"Proud of you two," Kyle pointed to Jessica and John, then explained to me, "it's a song from the film."

"We're a big fan of the classics around here."

"Raising 'em right," he nodded his approval.

"Will we see you tomorrow Ms. Evans?" one of the girls—Olivia I think—asked.

"Um, I'm not sure?" I looked at Jessica and John.

"Skates, Mates, and Carols!"

"And that is . . . ?" I turned to Kyle.

"Also on the list. Ice skating, snowman building, carols at the gazebo."

"Are you kidding me? Yet another event people would fall in love with."

Kyle leaned in conspiratorially. "Getting you to fall in love is the point . . . "

My stomach made a nervous flip.

"This town is something special. That's why I'm working so hard to get Grover to stop being so stubborn and accept certain changes and new endeavors. A lot of the town's population is aging, and we could use some assistance with our tax base."

An immediate drop at the realization he meant fall in love with the town, not him. Or did he?

John clapped Kyle on the shoulder. "Always thinking of the town, Kyle. When are you going to be our town manager?"

Kyle let out a slight sigh. "You know that's complicated. Well Ms. Evans, night is upon us. What do you say we get to our movie?"

He held out his hand, and tumultuous insides be damned, I placed mine on top and let him lead me away from the Sweet family and their festive village.

27

Back at the house my nerves started to bubble up again. It felt like my stomach was doing flips, and clearly I was no good at hiding my emotions around Kyle.

"I'm not going to jump you, you know," he said as he got out of the truck. And in true confusing-Charity manner, I simultaneously felt relief and disappointment. "I mean, unless you want me to," he added with a wink before shutting his door.

I hurried out after him and decided I'd ignore that last bit as we headed inside, even though I kind of, sort of, really *did* want him to jump me, especially after all our interrupted moments. The day felt like the longest round of foreplay known to mankind. It certainly was for me. Then again, I wasn't historically one for that anyway, often cut as another timesaving measure. But perhaps these were all changes that happened when you were finally lit up, which was something I could admit Kyle abso-freaken-lutely did to me. I looked at the snow all around and resisted the sudden urge to jump into it as a way to cool off.

"Just give me a few minutes to get everything set up," he said as we stepped inside.

"What's there to set up? Don't we just press play?"

Kyle looked at me like I had two heads. "This is no ordinary movie, Ms. Evans."

I started to realize he tended to say my name like that when he was trying to be stern. And I liked it. So instead of correcting him, I raised my eyebrows in question.

"Ok then, what can I do to help?"

"Go upstairs and put on that flannel nightgown."

"Excuse me?!"

"It gets cold in the living room. And this is supposed to be a festive and cozy event. We'll have to open up one of our gifts from my mom, too, but I'm sure she won't mind. They're an appropriate accessory."

"You can't be serious."

"What's wrong, Ms. Evans? Worried the sight of you in all that flannel will send me over the edge? I promise I'll be an upstanding gentleman."

My mind did that thing again and waffled between relief and a desire for him to be decidedly un-gentlemanly. "Does this mean you're going to don a nightshirt and cap?"

"Um, no. No, I'm not Mr. Scrooge. But I'll be similarly comfortable, I promise. Off with you now!"

I gave him a look as he all but shooed me toward the stairs, but I obliged and went to shower and change. When I returned, he'd made miraculous edits to the living room.

The ground in front of the sofa and chairs was filled with blankets and pillows all arranged to face the TV, which had the crackling fireplace on the left, and the glowing Christmas tree to the right. There was a snack tray similar to those Mary made on top of the blankets, along with mugs of cocoa. Kyle stood in flannel pajama pants and coordinating navy shirt, setting up the movie. I stood in the doorway and watched for a moment, much like I had the day they were decorating the tree. He was whistling a Christmas tune, and it was another I actually knew.

"With candy canes and silver lanes that glow," I finished along with him, which made him turn to me with a grin. "It's definitely starting to look like Christmas. I feel like I'm standing in a make-believe holiday house.

"I assure you, this is all very real," he said as he stepped closer and held out his hand like when we'd left the Sweet's. "What do you think? Too much? Or have I converted you to Cheerful Cherry?"

I screwed up my mouth like I was in serious contemplation as I let him lead me to the cozy floor bed.

"I mean, would we have called me grumpy before?" I asked as I settled myself on the fluffy comforter.

"Fair enough. Not grumpy, just dedicated. Focused. Slightly high-strung. Definitely not festive."

I laughed at his assessment, even though his astute observations remained a little unnerving.

"I'll give you some of those," I said as I accepted my cocoa. "But if I was ever high-strung it was only a byproduct of the snowy crash and uncertainty surrounding the big Wedding That Wasn't. I'd like to think I've since relaxed. I've certainly embraced the Christmas spirit considering prior years it was practically nonexistent."

Kyle stretched out beside me, his back against the pile of pillows he'd set in front of the sofa so we could lean against it and watch the movie.

"And why, exactly, was that?" he wondered before he took a sip of his drink and let out an involuntary moan. "Ah. That first sip always hits just right. And don't try to tell me it's just because you're a workaholic like you alluded to before, because honestly I don't completely buy it."

I shook my head in a mix of wonder and amusement at the joy he found in steamed milk and chocolate, and took a drink from my own mug before answering. He'd spiked it with peppermint schnapps, and the adult addition was delightful.

"We stopped celebrating Christmas like this—with an array of festive events, a tree at home, dinner, endless traditions—once my dad died. He absolutely loved the season, did I ever mention that? And I know now how much of the joy from this time of year came from him. He was so dang jolly. It felt like he was almost always laughing, and he loved making his family happy."

I turned my gaze to the fireplace and watched the dancing flames.

"The first Christmas it just didn't feel right without him. We said we'd try again the next year, but it didn't happen then either; mom suggested we go away instead. We figured the home we'd shared—a place with happy memories but its fair share of sad ones, the home where he lived and laughed but ultimately faded away and died—was too heavy a place for new, cheerful memories. So the three of us took a Christmas cruise, and once was enough for me. When I wasn't seasick, I was bored. And sad. It just didn't feel like Christmas captive in a glorified floating casino with thousands of strangers on the open ocean. I realized then maybe it would never feel like it once had. So the year after that I stayed behind. The house was sold, but some of that weight moved with us: we haven't had a traditional at-home Christmas since. In fact, I haven't spent Christmas with my family since that cruise, either. They kept traveling, alternating between cruises and trips. My mom met someone on one of them, and they're married now. My brother joined the military, got married, and now has two kids of his own, but they move around. As for me, my answer to the change in holidays was to forget about it. At least . . . forget about celebrating it myself. I'll help others enjoy this time of year through my work, but mostly I just like to keep busy until it passes by one checklist at a time."

Kyle was quiet for a moment, his eyes on the muted menu screen in front of us that showed two couples dressed in festive red and white garb. He'd taken the candy cane from his mug and was sucking on the end pensively. It was admittedly a bit distracting.

"I hope you don't take this the wrong way Cherry . . . " he said finally, and my stomach tumbled. It was actually absurd how that nickname uttered from his lips made me feel. It was . . . playful. It was unlike me. Or perhaps it *was* like me, just a version I'd kept buried deep.

"I think you've got it all wrong," he continued. "Losing your dad, I mean . . . of course it was a terrible, heartbreaking, life-altering thing to experience, and it fucking sucks that it happened to you. But giving up —or giving up *on*—the things he loved best because of it? That's the saddest thing of all. He loved Christmas. He loved his family. He loved to laugh. And I'm gonna go ahead and guess he loved *life*. So don't you think he'd want you to enjoy it? You can honor him that way, just like Jessica honors her sister with the Christmas village, and we honor my dad by daring to still ride snowmobiles through snowy nights, and loving on this town the same way he always did. And I don't mean enjoying life by racing *through* life. I mean by pausing. By sitting in a breakfast nook watching a cardinal's flight. By sneaking dough when you're baking Christmas cookies. Singing carols despite any concern you'll be off key. Noticing how crisp the stars look on a cold winter's night. Kissing 'cause the moment's right, and not because it's on a damn to-do list. "

I turned to find he wasn't looking at the screen anymore but at me, his eyes twinkling extra thanks to the flickering flames. My lips started tingling from the memory of our kisses, and I started to feel fluttery at the thought of another.

"I think you're right," I said, my voice barely more than a whisper. And I was *almost* certain I meant it, even if my heart hammered furiously at his gentle yet firm urging and a million different versions of "yeah but what if . . . " threatened to loop.

He nodded his approval at my response and leaned toward me, gaze flicking to my mouth and back again.

"Are we gonna watch the movie?" I asked, slightly breathless.

"Bing and Danny aren't going anywhere . . . " he took the candy cane from his mouth and pressed his lips to mine. His kiss tasted like peppermint, and I knew no matter what the future held, from now on I'd forever associate the flavor with him. With this night.

28

He was gone. I opened my eyes to find the television off, the fire died down, the snack tray and mugs cleared away. The Christmas tree continued to glow, now coupled with early morning light that filtered through cracks in the living room blinds.

Disappointment enveloped me as a result of his absence. The night had been one to remember, and while White Christmas was as lovely as I was promised it would be, it was definitely the performance before and the encore after I enjoyed the most.

Kyle and I fell asleep tangled up together, something else that was new for me. Darren and I could have kept a board down the middle of our bed—we typically stayed on our own sides. But there wasn't a single moment last night when Kyle and I weren't touching, when my head wasn't resting on his chest, or he hadn't wrapped an arm around me and tugged me against him. That is, a single moment until now, and his absence was keenly felt.

I stood, and as the flannel of the nightgown brushed my legs I thought of Kyle's roaming hands moving up, up, up beneath the fabric. I folded the blankets and stacked the pillows before walking around and confirming no one else was home. I showered and dressed in the silence, mulling over all that'd transpired in the last three and a half days. It felt impossible that so much had taken place; so many conversations, introductions, festive doings, laughs . . . and feelings.

In the kitchen I discovered Kyle brewed coffee before he left. The Santa mug I remembered him using that very first morning was left next to the machine alongside packets of cocoa mix, a bottle of festive sprinkles, and a note tucked underneath.

No plain lattes allowed. Mix a packet of cocoa in your coffee. Whipped cream in the fridge. Top with sprinkles. I wish I got to make it for you, but duty called. X

I smiled and followed his instructions, then took my drink to the island. It was so quiet I could hear the *tick, tock, tick, tock* of a nearby clock. I looked out the windows at another morning of sunshine, blue sky, and sparkling snow. It felt strange being here with no one else. The welcoming feelings were missing without Mary and Kyle, and in their stead I felt like exactly what I was: an unexpected guest in someone's home. Their absence threatened to let old worries creep in. Feelings shifted without them because that's what happened when you grew close to people and tied the two together. Wasn't it safer to keep your distance? To stick by hard and fast rules? To keep emotions tempered, if not separate from others altogether? If I was at my apartment, I wouldn't have given a second thought to waking up alone, because that was my usual state. Even being together as long as we were, Darren and I kept our own places.

But this experience was completely different from anything related to my ex. If only he knew what a wrench he'd thrown into my life with his sudden breakup. If only he knew the chain of events that followed. I sipped my drink and tried to focus on the night before; there was no reason to discount all that transpired just because I was alone when I woke. Mary was with her sister. Kyle had things to do. It was Monday, after all. I'd never specifically asked him what he did outside his role on the council—all I recalled were comments related to real estate. He could be at work, for all I knew. Heck, if this were any other Monday *I* would be at work. There were rational reasons I was alone.

I glanced around the beautiful kitchen and recalled our time sitting in the breakfast nook, the baking session, the singing, the banter and flirtations. There was no reason for me to discount those things just because I was sitting in silence, letting my mind whir with no work as distraction.

Another sip of mocha, and my eyes landed on the Christmas list left on the island as instructed. It rested on a Lazy Susan decorated for the season, underneath salt and pepper shakers that looked like Mr. and Mrs. Claus.

I picked it up and scanned the items, smiling at Kyle's tiny paintings. We'd done quite a few of them—plus several too personal to list—but there were more remaining: build a snowman, go ice skating, carols at the gazebo, Christmas Eve Fete . . .

And then, tucked toward the bottom, one more I'd never seen before, written in a frame painted to look like Christmas ribbon tied on top with a bow.

Fall in love this Christmas?

The question made my heart skip a beat. Fall in love with *what*? Or *who*? He'd left out the noun. With Christmas? With life? With *him*? All the above? The possibilities filled me with excitement. My stomach fluttered and I felt a sense of elation and then . . .

Anxiety came to play. My feels made a 180. Racing heart, not happy little skip. Nervous flutters. Clammy hands. Weighted, not elated. I started second guessing everything. Instead of excitement, angst at Kyle's suggestions I pause more, live more, embrace the season—lean into the things I'd kept at bay in response to the ache of loss.

Maybe it was time for me to go. I'd driven my car to the house after our visit with the Sweets, and Jackie was now in the driveway ready and waiting. This was all too much, wasn't it? To go from workaholic Charity Evans with everything in complete control to this woman who got swept away in a quaint Christmas town? I didn't say yes to spontaneity. I didn't say yes to feelings that set me on fire.

My anxiety put me on autopilot and I washed my mug, tidied up the bedroom, gathered my belongings and brought them to Jackie in record time. I slammed the trunk, returned to the house for my bag, abdd paused in the living room to admire our tree one last time. And then I heard a familiar voice.

"Hello? Charity?"

Mary.

"Oh, Charityyyyyy!"

This voice, bubbly and sing-song, had to be Emmeline.

I stepped out from the living room to find them in the entryway. Emmeline gave me a hug and slinked an arm around my waist. "I'm so glad you're already up and dressed! Are you ready to go? Did you know we were on our way?"

"I . . . no, actually."

"Oh, Kyle." Mary shook her head. "He's got so much on his mind lately. Seems he forget to tell you."

"And by 'so much on his mind' she means *you*," Emmeline laughed.

"Well, yes. There's that, but you know that's not all," Mary added. "Well, shall we?" She motioned toward the door. "I noticed your car is already running. Do you want to drive?"

I held up my hands. "Wait, wait, I don't even know what we're doing!"

"Oh, right! Well, since Kyle is at work, we didn't want to leave you hanging around here with nothing to do," Emmeline said as she walked me toward the door. "So we figured we'd have breakfast with some old folks then tackle the Angel Tree!"

"I'm sorry . . . what??"

"Come on, I'll explain on the way. I'm totally down with taking the Bimmer, by the way" Emmeline added. "Fancy!"

And so, instead of hightailing it out of Auburn Falls in a fit of anxiety, I found myself heading back to town with Emmeline and Mary on an adventure I didn't quite comprehend.

29

Everything was soon made clear.

It turned out, perhaps unsurprisingly, that Kyle wasn't the only civic-minded member of the Morrison family.

"Mom instilled the importance of service from a young age," Emmeline explained as we parked outside the community center. "I can't remember a time when we weren't participating in some sort of volunteer effort, especially around the holidays. The senior breakfast is something I do year-round, though. There's a bookclub here as well that I'm part of. I just think the older folks are so dang interesting. They've experienced so much, have plenty of stories to tell, and I get a kick out of the way they're still very much *alive*, if you know what I mean; they joke around and flirt with each other and it's hilarious to watch."

"Great food and great company," Mary added. "I don't think every senior breakfast can boast both, but here in Auburn Falls we've got it right."

"It's going to be extra amazing today being the last meal before Christmas!" Emmeline announced happily.

From the outside, the community center looked like a grand, historic manor house. But inside the impact of Grover's donation was apparent, as everything was stylish and updated. In the festively decorated dining room, a majority of the tables were already filled and delicious scents wafted through the air.

"Lottie always makes pastries for the breakfast," Mary explained. "She opens late on Mondays, too, so she can help cook. I'll be in the kitchen with her, but you can stay out here with Emmeline and enjoy the company—and food."

As if on cue, several people called out to Emmeline to join them. Unexpectedly, I heard "Snowstorm Girl!" hollered by a few breakfast-goers as well.

"Come on, I'm starving!" Emmeline said with a smile as I followed her to some seats.

❄❄❄

Neither of them exaggerated. Breakfast was delicious, and the conversation was lively and amusing. We sat at a table with several others, two of whom Emmeline whispered got caught kissing in the storage closet last year.

As we drove away a couple hours later with full hearts and bellies, I silently chided myself for my almost-departure without saying goodbye. These two continued to be so wonderful, they didn't deserve that. And being with them, I had to admit, was like a balm. Like Kyle, their friendly, easy-going manner was contagious, and I felt relaxed in their presence.

"I'm so glad I met you both. I genuinely appreciate how welcoming you've been, and all you've done for me. I'll never forget it."

"Well that was out of the blue and sounds an awful lot like a goodbye, Charity," Mary said. "Do you know something we don't?"

"I just wanted to make sure you knew," I said, relying on a half-truth. "I'm likely to get distracted when we're shopping. Did you know it's a favorite pastime?"

Another half-truth. It'd been a long time since I did any in-store shopping. I usually relied on the internet, but I was looking forward to it today. On the way out of the center we'd stopped by the Angel Tree in the foyer. I'd learned it was a tabletop tree filled with tags that listed the name and age of someone in the area who could use help with gifts that year, alongside the things they'd like. Or, rather, the tree was filled with tags at the *start* of the season, but as we neared, Emmeline and Mary were thrilled to discover not a single tag remained.

"We did a couple earlier in the month, but I always like to make sure none are left behind. There were still a few at the end of last week," Emmeline explained.

"Wait!" I said, as I noticed the corner of a piece of paper toward the top of the tree mostly hidden in the boughs. I snagged the single tag.

"Oh dear, I'm so glad you noticed that!" Mary said.

"Me too," Emmeline added. "Could you imagine being the only one who didn't get their tag fulfilled?!"

"Well then, let's get to it!" I said with enthusiasm.

And that was how we'd started our shopping excursion, which took me outside Auburn Falls for the first time since Thursday. We sang along to Christmas songs as we drove half an hour south to a town that lacked the charm I'd been experiencing, but boasted all the chain stores I was used to. I had to admit it felt weird being surrounded by hustle and bustle and brand names again after days in a small town with local stores. I felt like I was waking from a dream, and part of me worried both my companions would vanish into thin air for leaving the confines of their town, but no such thing occurred.

At the sight of a well-known coffee shop, I couldn't help but detour to the drive-thru for one of my standard lattes, but I let out a disgusted sigh after taking a sip that had Mary and Emmeline laughing.

"Ruined forever. Thanks Lottie!"

The morning passed in a whirl of shopping and laughter, and we headed back to town in the early afternoon after stopping for lunch with a trunk full of bags. We dropped the gifts at the center for delivery and headed straight to the town green for Skates, Mates, and Carols.

School was out for the week, and the snowy expanse was already filled with children running around throwing snowballs and playing. The center of the green featured a classic white gazebo with a giant pine tree beside it, and I was told both would light up when the sun set in a couple hours.

"What do you say? Do you wanna build a snowman?" Emmeline asked in her sing-song way. Mary already headed off with her friend-not-beau Tom.

I was about to say yes, but someone else answered before me.

"Settle down, Anna, she's with me."

My heart skipped a beat at the sound of Kyle's voice, and I turned to find him smiling at me, a to-go cup in each hand.

"Ugh. Fineeee. See ya Charity, I had fun with you this morning!" She gave me a hug then wandered away.

"Why'd you call her Anna?"

Another look of disbelief from Kyle. "Because she sang the question like Anna from *Frozen* . . . ? Nevermind. Have some cocoa." He chuckled and handed me a cup. "Snowman or skating first?"

"Oh wow, we're really doing all that?"

"We're really doing all that," he confirmed with a smirk. "It's on the list!"

At his mention of the list, I remembered the final item he'd added and was certain he'd be able to hear my heart thrumming against my chest if we were in a quieter location.

Fall in love this Christmas . . .

I wanted desperately to ask him what he meant, but I was also totally terrified at the possible answer.

"Happy to see you've got gloves this time," he said, leaving no time for a mental spiral.

"I do! And how about this hat, ey? Emmeline found it while we were shopping and insisted. She can be very persuasive."

Kyle looked at the sparkly, pink pom-pom hat. "That's a nice way to put it. And it's adorable. You look extra kissable in it, actually."

To prove his point, he leaned over and placed a light kiss on my lips that immediately put my senses on high alert.

"I'm sorry I wasn't there this morning," he said as he pulled away. "I had a bit of work to get done at the office, and needed to chat with Grover. About the Christmas Eve party, actually."

"What about it?"

"He wasn't thrilled at not being consulted on the changes."

"Did he need to be consulted?"

"Oh absolutely not, but you remember what I said about him being resistant to change. He likes to be in control, too." Kyle paused. "Huh."

"What?" I asked, even though I had a feeling I knew what he was about to say.

"Kind of reminds me of you in that way, actually."

I swatted him playfully on the shoulder.

"Kyle Morrison, did you just compare me to a grumpy old man?"

"Hey, if the title fits . . . and you called me a grandpa before so now we're even. Maybe I should set a meeting between the two of you."

I rolled my eyes. "Go ahead, I could turn on the charm and melt him faster than an icicle in a bonfire."

"Oh I don't doubt it. But that's also my uncle we're talking about, so then again maybe not. For now at least let's just focus on the activities at hand. To my earlier question: skates or mates?"

"Hmm . . . mates," I finally decided, and we headed to join the snowman building party, leaving worries about unanswered questions and grumpy town managers behind.

30

The green was filled with an army of snowmen, women, and children, and actual people were scattered between them, waiting for carols to start. After creating our own snowy figure, Kyle and I tried our hand at skating on the small rink made courtesy of the fire department. I completed a few rounds holding tight to his hand, but we decided soon after to leave the ice to the daredevil youth zipping around us.

The sun was just below the horizon, and both tree and gazebo were lit as promised, their festive lights glowing in the dusk. Most everyone gathered by the latter where the church choir stood to lead the singing. Unlit candles were passed around, and soon several small flames began to flicker, and the number quickly grew as people used their own candles to light their neighbor's. Before long, the place seemed filled with fallen stars, and the choir began to sing. When the first refrain of "Silent Night" filled the air and the volume increased as the crowd joined in, an unexpected wave of emotion hit me.

All is calm, all is bright . . .

Tears filled my eyes at the sight and sound. I was completely blindsided by the beauty of the event. The emotion that filled me felt stronger than anything I'd experienced before. . . . No. That wasn't true; I'd felt heartache this acute, but tonight instead of a constricting pain, the emotion felt expansive and light. I felt like the Grinch at the end of the classic story—another I actually remembered from my childhood—when his heart grew three sizes at the realization Christmas was about love and togetherness, not material goods.

And that was precisely what I was experiencing now, wasn't it? Amid the glow of candles, the sweet refrain of carols, friendship and community, and the possibility of a relationship that lit me up, I was discovering *life* was about love and togetherness, if only I could let go enough to let in the unexpected. If only I was *brave enough* to let it in.

Was I brave?

Kyle brought a thumb to my cheek and wiped away a tear. I looked at him, somehow even more handsome in the soft glow of candlelight, and the whir of emotions I'd felt the entire time I'd been here hummed beneath the surface. This was all so beautiful. So magical. But how did I know it was true? How could I be sure I wasn't caught up in the charm of Auburn Falls at Christmas and the mirth—and fire—of the man beside me? I thought of the way being in another town today made me feel like I was waking from a dream. I needed to discern what was real.

I leaned toward Kyle and pressed a kiss against his lips. Tonight he tasted like cocoa. I savored the sensation for a moment then pulled away. I smiled at him softly, hoping to convey a silent "everything is fine."

And then . . . I left.

❄❄❄

I walked into my showcase-worthy apartment and let the door shut behind me. It closed with a slam and click that seemed to echo throughout the wide, open space. Wide and open. Two terms I'd used to describe Kyle's barn, yet despite being without heat it didn't feel nearly as cold as this. Had it always felt that way?

Whether Kyle thought I was going for a cocoa refill or a bathroom break, or he knew I was leaving and decided to let me go I didn't know, but he didn't follow as I made my way through the throng of carolers. And the last thing I heard before driving away was refrains of "The First Noel" filling the air.

Now back in Boston after a drive that made me feel less festive— that deflated some of the elation I'd felt during the carols—with every mile, I showered and hoped hot water would clear my head and recenter me in my world. Instead, it gave me more time to think, and it wasn't work thoughts that filled my mind per usual. It was a swirl of thoughts about a small town nestled beside a mountain; of a cozy brick house and a woman with a kind smile. Friendly townsfolk. Baking cookies. Laughter. Fresh cut Christmas trees. Amber eyes and a signature smirk with a single dimple. Mochas and hot cocoa. Mistletoe. Cinnamon bun shares. Snowmobiles, S'mores, and starry skies. Polar

Plunges. Falling snow. Cuddles—and more—by the fire.

I turned off the water and gave my head a literal shake, like my mind would clear alongside the flying droplets. It didn't work.

I donned cozy sweats and a tee, tossed my hair in a bun, and went to my room to unpack. I'd always been prompt with that sort of thing, and tonight would be no exception. I unzipped my suitcase and let out a sound of disgust at the haphazard way I'd tossed everything in. I started to sort the clothes into piles but paused when I moved aside the cashmere sweater from that very first day and came across Kyle's sweatshirt: the evergreen one I'd grabbed from the back of his truck and meant to return.

I'd forgotten it after our tree hunt. I held it against my nose, and the power of scent did its thing, transporting me back to Auburn Falls and our time together. I warmed as I thought of the way his hands felt as they roamed my body, and the way we fit together.

I slipped the sweatshirt over my head, poured a large glass of wine, and went to the living room. I sat on my pristine cream-colored leather couch and turned the TV to a fireplace simulation. I pulled up my knees, tucked them under the sweatshirt, and stared at the faux flame. It was a far cry from the ambiance I'd experienced over the last few days, but it was better this way, wasn't it?

After all, this is what I knew. This is what was real.

31

6 AM

I just needed to get back to my routine. At least, that's what I told myself as I got out of bed after waking to Bill Withers' voice, exactly like I was supposed to. I followed my usual routines to the T, and added a few extra lists for good measure. Did I need to write down the steps for making coffee? Absolutely not. Did I do it anyway? Abso-freaken-lutely. Did I need to write down the workout order I rarely altered before heading to my building's gym? Nope. Did I do it anyway? Yep. Did I need a list for shower, hair, or makeup routine? Definitely not, yet here I was, checking off the final item on the latter after lip balm application.

Finishing lists still left me feeling gratified, but now I heard a snarky little voice in my head that said things like, "Yeah but there are better roads to gratification if you know what I mean…" This was inevitably followed by flashes of moments with a small-town councilman. I tried desperately to ignore them.

9 AM

I opted to work from home for the day and headed to my office with a protein shake. I preferred a green smoothie, but my time away meant a lack of fresh produce. I let out a sigh as the first sip of what was typically a very satisfactory meal just made me think of Lottie's cinnamon buns. And a cinnamon bun my vanilla shake was *not*, despite the pinch of the spice I'd mixed in. By the time I begrudgingly finished, I was annoyed at past me for being so dang organized. I researched potential vendors and venues to add to our roster, went over a few of my spreadsheets, checked our calendar for the upcoming year, and let excitement course through me at the thought of the different events we already had scheduled.

I paid close attention to how these tasks made me feel as I tried to work my way through the morning. My time away didn't make me like what I did any less, thank goodness, and I found I had in fact missed the routine of it all. The thing was . . . I missed the experiences in Auburn Falls, too. I tried my hardest to keep thoughts of that place at bay. Hadn't that been the point in leaving? Get away to discern reality from Christmas magic. That was the goal.

But there wasn't nearly enough to do to occupy my time or my mind. Even my inbox was neat and orderly, with only a handful of emails to sort; the end of year was always quiet. I was thrilled, however, to find not only a few event inquiries that mentioned the Hannigan wedding among the usual promotional emails, but several requests for comment Re: The I Do's That Didn't from gossip publications and entertainment shows. Both called for discussion with Natalie, and I was ecstatic our hopes for publicity from the event were coming true as I gave her a call.

But for the first time in five years she didn't pick up. My concern was immediate yet short-lived as I remembered giving her time off. I smiled at the thought of her enjoying the holidays somewhere, with people she cared so much about she wouldn't pause to answer a call. Meanwhile, I was on track to celebrate alone. True, it was my own doing, and I could—should?—follow the ways of past me and nix the festivities entirely. But I could already admit that at the very least, my time surrounded by the charm and cheer of Auburn Falls reignited my own desire to enjoy the season. *You could honor him that way.* I heard Kyle's words in my head, and while I remained worried about unwittingly donning rose-colored glasses—Kyle would probably say cranberry-colored was more appropriate this time of year—I could admit he'd been right about a lot, including the way I handled things that reminded me of dad.

Now, I looked forward to time spent with family in the coming years, and to putting a little more holly jolly on the calendar moving forward. I found myself wondering if mom still had the recipe for the snickerdoodles I randomly remembered dad loving, or his favorite corn casserole I'd scoffed at as a child. Maybe I could try my hand at making both—a confidence in the kitchen given to me by Mary. But none of that would help this year.

I rearranged my desk for the fourth time, and rolled my eyes as I picked up the faux plant I'd had since forever. It suddenly seemed ridiculous I wouldn't even commit to keeping a plant alive.

11 AM

I let out an annoyed sigh and pushed away from my desk. I'd give myself an early lunch. I was in charge, after all. I could do that sort of thing. In the immaculate, rarely-used kitchen, I rummaged for something to eat and came up empty-handed. Another shake, granola with no milk to go with it, a protein bar, frozen shrimp and vegetables . . . I didn't want any of those things.

I thought of a restaurant, cream-colored with dark wood accents. Fairy lights and a fireplace. Friendly conversation, shirt sleeves rolled the to elbows . . . and shepherd's pie.

I shook my head. I didn't need to be in a secluded town for all that, this was Boston after all. I grabbed my coat, donned a scarf and gloves, and headed outside.

11:30 AM

Had I been living here in a daze? I'd been worried my time in Auburn Falls and the Christmas cheer it provided had put me in a dreamlike stupor. Yet now, walking down Newbury Street a couple days before Christmas it almost felt like that's what I'd been in all along. I felt like I was seeing things for the first time. Had the majority of the shops always been decorated like this? Had there always been this many people, arms laden with Christmas packages, happily chatting as they wandered the streets clutching warm beverages? Apparently my laser-focus made me miss quite a lot. There was a different kind of festive feel here, but it was still lovely. I smiled to myself as I looked around. No, a few days in a small town didn't suddenly make me hate life in the city. Boston was a special place.

I stopped at a nearby famous bakery, where I was disappointed to learn they only had buns on the weekends, but treated myself to a cinnamon scone instead. It was delicious, undeniably so, yet it didn't keep me from missing Lottie's—not just the baked goods, but the design of the place. I found I preferred the cozy pink details to the industrial kitchen-like vibes of this one.

I inhaled a breath of crisp air as I continued on my way. I passed the chain coffeeshop where Natalie typically bought my latte, but instead of going in, I made my way to a local spot I vaguely recalled being across the street from my favorite gift shop. The shop with my pine scented candle.

I was rewarded by my decision when I entered the tiny café to find a chalkboard decorated in festive images—which made me think of Kyle's art on the Christmas list, of course—with a variety of holiday-themed beverages. I wouldn't say plain lattes would forever be a thing of the past, but I was certainly willing to savor drinks with a bit more pizazz now. I ordered a mistletoe mocha.

Now feeling much like the rest of the holiday shoppers, I crossed the street and entered The Velvet Bow. I beelined for my pine candle, then discovered I could—and wanted to—browse a while. Perhaps I'd actually find a few gifts for people. They certainly wouldn't reach my mom or my brother and his family before the holiday, but what was the saying? It's the thought that counts. I'd do better next year.

1 PM

So much for my plan for an early lunch. Arms laden with my own bags full of gifts I was excited to distribute, I got out of my rideshare in front of the Irish restaurant I'd found on Beacon Street.

I headed in for my shepherd's pie and found myself in a place that boasted dark wood, cream walls, and decorations much like The Hearth, but decor that was decidedly Irish-themed. The plethora of paintings and photographs that covered several areas were highlighted by dark green accent walls.

As I took a seat in one of the booths, two things hit me: 1. I was being spontaneous, and 2. I'd left my place without laptop or notebooks. As a result, I was left with bags full of presents and nothing to do but practice presence as I enjoyed my meal.

3 PM

Overall, I was proud of the way I'd been handling the day. I'd done quite a bit, yet when I looked at the clock on the wall back at my apartment, I was surprised at the time. Why was it moving so slow? Unsure what else to do, I rearranged the furniture in the living room.

4 PM

I started to question my decision to leave. At the very least, I questioned the way I'd slinked off like a thief in the night instead of telling Kyle I needed time to think like an actual adult. I wanted to call him. To explain things. But as I picked up my phone I realized we'd never exchanged numbers. We were together practically the entire time with no need to text or call. Getting his number just never come up.

I blew out a breath and looked around my living room, hands on hips. I went to my bedroom, pulled off the duvet and pillows, and tossed them on the floor in front of the sofa. The decorative pillows from the couch went next. It was a far cry from the arrangement Kyle had made; it looked more like a mess than anything intentional, and was missing snacks, a Christmas tree, a blazing fire . . . and a warm body to cozy up against.

Even so, it would have to do. I changed into comfy clothes, donned a face treatment, ordered from my favorite sushi restaurant, and put on *White Christmas*.

7 PM

The highlight of the evening was scaring the delivery person. I'd forgotten about the mask the same hue as the seaweed wrapped around my dinner, and when I opened the door, the way he jumped made *me* jump, and then we both dissolved into a fit of laughter. Embarrassment might have been my reaction in the past, but now . . . now I just thought of what Kyle would have said if he was with me. Likely some comment about ghost stories around Christmastime and how a jump scare was actually fitting. It was one of the tangents he'd gone on while I was there.

"You know A Christmas Carol is a *ghost story*, right?"

I smiled at the memory.

But apart from that little moment, my sushi-for-one and encore viewing of *White Christmas* was a little lackluster. I still enjoyed both, the way I still liked just about everything I'd done during the day, and yet . . . now it didn't quite feel like enough, and I found myself feeling glum.

I'd wondered at my bravery while listening to the carols, but my abrupt departure answered the question for me: not brave, fucking terrified. Was giving into that fear worth it? Had I made the right decision?

I groaned and put myself to bed early.

32

It was the candle that confirmed I was wrong.

I woke up Christmas Eve Day, lit my pine scented candle, and stared at it while I sipped coffee. Plain coffee. I had no cocoa packets.

I put a Christmas scene on the TV, and while it contained a tree and crackling fire and some instrumental holiday tracks, it did nothing to spark a festive mood. In fact, it felt . . . well, pathetic. And entirely *not* real.

The tree I'd picked out at Mr. Fuller's farm? Real. The fireplace Kyle laid me down in front of? Real. The things I felt when his mouth and hands roamed over my skin? Definitely real.

Scent from my pine tree candle? Fake as fuck.

Putting some distance between myself and Auburn Falls hadn't shown me all that transpired there was some pretend, Christmas-magic induced dream. On the contrary, as the pine fragrance started to fill my apartment, I realized being in that town and with those people had actually shown me the ways I was going through my life in Boston in a dream-like manner. My stroll through the streets yesterday proved that. I prided myself on my attention to detail when it came to my company's events, yet I was missing out on some of the details in my own life.

And yes, it was true, fear was in part to blame. It was probably apparent to more people than I realized, but Kyle was the first to say it to my face.

You call it control, but I call it fear . . . you've gotta let people in, Charity.

Damnit, but that man was right. I'd spent years pushing away meaningful relationships—with my mom and John, my brother and his family, potential friends—and settling for a cool sort of

180

companionship where there should be fire because of those fears.

But maybe it was time to get the hell over it.

Fall in love this Christmas . . .

I loved my work and was oh-so-proud of my company, but I could see now how I'd also used my career and busyness to keep relationships at a safe distance. Surely I didn't need to keep doing that; I didn't need to use my work to keep out love, just like letting in love didn't mean I had to sacrifice my work. Certainly both were possible. Balance. Wasn't that the goal?

A sudden vision of my dad came to mind. I had a feeling if he were here he'd be nodding along at all my admissions.

"Atta girl," he'd likely say. "Proud of you."

I smiled to myself and thought about sitting down to make a list. Perhaps this was a good time for some pros and cons, or columns of "real" vs "unreal." But as I headed for my trusty notebook, I decided to do something else instead. Something unexpected. I was learning, after all, that there were times the unexpected led to the best gifts of all. So instead of grabbing my pens and starting to write, I opened my desk drawer and slid the items inside.

"Just for now," I assured them as I pushed it shut. Then I looked at my watch and headed for the door. I could only hope I'd find an open store and all the ingredients I needed . . .

❄❄❄

Deja vous struck as I crested Dog Hill and white flecks appeared in my headlights. It was snowing again. On Christmas Eve. Could this place be anymore perfect? But unlike my first foray into Auburn Falls, it was excitement that filled my belly tonight. Excitement and hope. And, okay, maybe a *little* fear Kyle wouldn't forgive my abrupt departure or would look at me like a bug in his mug of cocoa. But I refused to dwell on those possibilities. I was ready to accept more risk in my life; I wanted the gains that came with it.

The church was a beacon in the winter night, its windows filled with candles that cast a warm glow in the dark. I inhaled a breath of crisp wintry air as I parked and stepped out of the car. It felt appropriate for me to wear the same heeled ankle boots from that very first night, but now they were paired with black tights and a red dress I kept on hand for holiday events.

I made my way into the building, ready to follow the sound of music and cheerful chatter down to the party, but I stopped abruptly and inhaled a sharp breath as Kyle came around the corner. He froze the same way I had.

"Kyle," I said, barely more than a whisper.

I watched him swallow. He looked ridiculously handsome in a black peacoat and jeans, and the sight of him made the day we'd been apart feel more like a year. I'd missed him.

"You came back," he said finally.

"I did," I acknowledged, as we stepped closer to each other. "Were you leaving?"

"I was. I didn't feel my usual cheer . . . not without you here, if I'm being honest."

"Kyle Morrison? Lacking cheer? Blasphemy."

"Yeah well . . . " he trailed off, his eyes moving somewhere behind me. "It hurt when I realized you'd gone, Charity. It was a little embarrassing, too. Everyone kept asking where you'd gone and I didn't have an answer. And then . . . well, you know about old wounds. After she learned I wasn't going to go along with her plans, Kelly left suddenly as well."

I felt like crying at the thought of the pain I'd caused by my selfish departure. Kyle was genuinely the most wonderful man I'd ever known apart from my dad. The thought of causing him hurt made *me* hurt.

"I'm so sorry, Kyle. For leaving the way that I did. It was childish and stupid. I believe I once called communication key and said it requires constant practice. This is definitely case in point." I brought a hand to his cheek. "You didn't deserve that. This will probably come as no surprise, but I was scared. Terrified, even. This all felt so wonderful, it might seem silly but I was afraid it was a dream. Like the magic of the season was playing tricks on me."

He brought his gaze back to mine. "You're easily the strongest, smartest, most dedicated and successful woman I know. Being scared doesn't suit you."

"Half the time I feel like I'm only acting at the things you mentioned. Inside I think I'm mainly just a sad, scared little girl. At least . . . that's what I've been until recently."

"And now?"

"Now I'm a little braver. Because of you. Because of this town."

He brushed a stray curl from my face and tucked it behind my ear. "Atta girl."

I smiled to myself as I recalled earlier when I'd imagined my dad saying the exact same thing. A spirit wink. There was comfort in that.

"I made you cookies," I said as I held up the plate wrapped in cellophane with a red bow on top. "No guarantees on flavor. First time solo."

Kyle's dimple flexed as he took the plate from my hands and placed it on a nearby bench after swiping the bow off the top. "Proud of you, Cherry, and appreciate the thought . . . " he said as he stepped back toward me. "But you're the gift I'd been hoping for, not a bunch of baked goods."

He gently pressed the bow on top of my head and I let out a laugh.

"Well? What do you think?" I asked. "Keep or return?"

He took one of my hands in his, wrapped an arm around my waist, and we started dancing to a song that drifted up from the party.

You can't tell me that Christmas gets better than this . . .

It felt so good to be near him again. To have our skin touching, and to inhale his signature scent from the source instead of an evergreen sweatshirt.

"Keep," he finally answered. "Definitely keep."

My heart fluttered happily. "Good. But I need you to know I'm not about to uproot my entire life for a man I spent less than a week with, no matter how fantastic and magical it was."

"Fair enough, I'd never ask you to anyway." He looked thoughtful for a moment. "So what's next?"

"Well, tonight we party. And then . . . how about planning on Christmas?"

That slow grin I was coming to adore spread across his face. He leaned in and answered with a kiss that sent tingles from my lips to the tips of my toes.

I had a feeling this was going to be a very merry Christmas.

The end

About the Author

Geeta Schrayter writes feel-good stories in quintessential New England settings. When she isn't putting happily ever after on the page, she can be found living out her own with her husband and children in Connecticut. She's forever working her way through an endless TBR and a notebook of book ideas, and loves connecting with readers.

Find her on social media:
instagram.com/geetawrites

Subscribe to her newsletter:
paperscrapstories.substack.com